We EXPECT THE DRIP

Not

the Downpour!

We EXPECT THE DRIP
Not
the Downpour!

I want to give special thanks to the wonderful people who helped inspire this novel. To my Lord and Savior, Yashua the Christ, thank you! To you, the reader, enjoy a great story.

My children, mommy loves. Family and friends, you are all in my heart. Shalom.

Table of Contents

It can feel like the rain pouring down has no other purpose than to beat you down. You've played the game, got the education, heard the prophecy, but what next? What do you do when your life doesn't mirror what you heard? Do you keep believing even if you do not see the promise fulfilled?

Is it our patience? Did we miss something or improperly hear, so we stand outside the will of Yah (God)? We look for the drip and expect the outpour! I heard this preached one day, listening to Dr. Krystal Lee. She was dynamic and energized, and her testimony moved me. I thought she was amazing, but I couldn't bring her story to reflect mine. I couldn't see myself in her story. I only saw lack and pain.

Have you ever heard a word that you wanted desperately to be your story? She said, "We look for the simple things and seek to build momentum with consistency. We don't doubt and always believe. We walk by faith and not by sight."

Wow, when she said that, I was mesmerized. My soul wanted to jump up and down and say that's it! I needed that–and I did. Furthermore, she said, "We are the salt of the earth, and we cannot lose our saltiness. If life is a drought or the rain is not seen in the clouds. If the water is a drizzle or a full-on downpour, the posture to move the Almighty is the same. In our weakness, He is made strong! If you lack vision, trust His plan for your life. When you feel like giving up, let the Word take the wheel! If doubt creeps in or naysayers attack your confidence, don't run, but double down!"

She spoke straight to me, and seeing and hearing it, I knew it was the power of Yah. This little woman had the power and conviction so intense I wanted what she had. Not her money and things, that's not a problem for me anyway. I wanted to garner her style of boldness and confidence. My life is more like a storm that never ends. I seemingly jump from one bad crisis to the next with hardly time to breathe. I desperately want to be set free, but I struggle to get off the dock!

I barely left the shore and want to sail into success, reach the deep blue sea, and see the world. Yet I have no passport and have only been shuffled around from family to family. If we were playing monkey in the middle, I would definitely be the monkey trying to grab ahold of the bold idea tossed over my head and sideways.

I want my life to change, and I needed to believe this sermon more than I knew she had the conviction to preach it. My life is like living on a dune. Every step is heavy and laborious. Something is constantly being stirred up and taking me by storm. The storm, the power of the wind with the sand, feels like sandpaper rubbing my face raw.

I am at a low place, yet I never seem to reach rock bottom enough. Whenever I am low, I seem to get lower, and the pain hurts. But just maybe I can believe and see what they–Yah even sees for me. The first Word I thought came from Heaven concerning me was so sweet, and even though I was young, I received it. So, I guess I should start there, and you can see where my life goes…

Noah said it was going to rain. But nobody believed him. They looked around and laughed at him when he decided to build a boat. They thought, how dumb can this man be to harp on and on about rain coming when we have been in a drought or never have seen such rain before? What makes Noah so special that God would let it rain for forty days and forty nights?

What made Noah so special to think he could spread around a message so ludicrous that anyone would pay him any attention? They thought he was crazy and wrote him off. They laughed all the more at him daily when they saw him spending money on something they didn't see a need to worry about. His time of preparation was not their time of worriment. They were living and doing everything under the sun.

But he kept telling them, believing, and building. Notice – it is not clear if his own family believed him. It's not recorded in the Bible that Noah had the help of his wife or sons to build the Ark. It doesn't record Noah having helpers, but he was faithful to build and used his resources to hire others who did help. How long the Ark took to complete is not important. The focal point is that Noah was faithful, and because of this, his family had room in the Ark, too! His favor extended to the family.

So now, back to me. I didn't get a message like Noah. I wasn't raised in a family where the righteousness of my mother or father gave me some special privilege. My parents met in a regular way, at a house party. My dad was hanging out with his college buddies, and my mom was fresh out of high school.

They were both good-looking, so it made sense they would lock eyes and have a conversation. Based on my experience with them, I imagine my mom was cunning and cute. She has a baby face, or so I have been told, and her puppy eyes get results. My dad was putty in her hands, and she liked it that way.

My dad wasn't a serial dater. He was really the quiet type. They say you have to watch out for the quiet ones, but with my father, he was as mild as they come. I can never remember him yelling and shouting when he lived with us. Not hearing the yelling made me very sensitive to when people raised their voices in conversations.

Perhaps my experiences hindered me because I didn't hear a fight here and there. Maybe I should have, and my parents would have stayed together like other miserable marriages. But my parents had their own thing going on. My dad and my mom dated for about six months before they decided to get married. I'm not sure if it was love on my mom's part or her desire to leave home that propelled her decision the most.

I wouldn't call my mother a golddigger, but she was definitely money-motivated. They were both young, and I am sure they had faults on both sides. So I am nobody's judge, but from what I heard, here's my mom's side.

"Gerald, what do you think? Do you like any of these styles? I feel like our wedding should be white, pink, and silver," says Kristina.

"I don't think we need no–pink wedding. That seems gay to me. I mean, what grown man wants a pink wedding? You can't just pick a different color like beige, black, or blue; something else in the rainbow without picking the rainbow?"

"Do you really think pink is gay? I know plenty of men who wear pink and are not gay. Of course, if we are getting married, you are not gay. I am not asking you to wear pink anyway. I am saying on the tables, the napkins and flowers can be pink. Then we can add some bling to make everything pop!"

"How much are we talking? I thought this was supposed to be simple, and we could do it big later?"

"I know this is simple. I wanted a carriage, a big hotel, and a getaway to Aruba. Now, what I would love is a destination wedding. But I understand we are on a budget, so if we can spend like ten thousand, we should be good."

"Ten thousand dollars? Are you crazy? I was thinking more like two or three thousand dollars."

"Stop playing; you know you can't get married for no dang two, three thousand dollars. This ain't the 60s or something. Prices have gone up. Just to book a decent venue is three thousand dollars, and then you gotta add the photographer and my dress. That doesn't even include the ring you are going to buy, either. That should be three months' salary or thereabout in case you need some guidance. But it's alright to splurge a little bit." She gives him a hug and a kiss while she jokes with him.

"Girl, you sure we don't need to wait on this? I wanted to get a car and get us a place. I thought we were taking this slow?"

"Look, if you want to get married, this is what it costs. Just let me know what you want to do."

"Yo, you know I want to get married and everything, but we have to get some things in position first."

"Fine, if you don't want to marry me, just say that. I am not begging any man to marry me. If you won't, I know the right one will. I just–"

"Fine, Kristina. I will figure it out. But I ain't wearing no pink."

"That's fine. You can wear white and you will match me, so not an issue. When can I start booking stuff?"

"Just give me a minute, and let me figure things out. I will let you know."

My mom hung up the phone, getting what she wanted–at least for the time being. My dad, on the other hand, had to make magic happen. He asked everybody in his family for money to get what he was short. He got up from the couch and went to his parents first. "Hey, Mom, how are you doing?"

"Good, son–how are you?" she replied, uncertain of his angle but knowing there was more behind the question. She sat down at the table to listen to him, and he sat opposite her. "I got to ask you for a favor."

She interrupts him, "Now, before you go asking for money, you know what your father will say. If you want money, you are going to have to work for

14

it. He is not giving you nothin' for free. You know I love you, but I can't have my husband mad at me. When you get married, you will understand."

Gerald shook his head, smirked, and said, "How did you know I was going to ask for money?" She smiled and replied, "A mother always knows when something is behind a 'Hey, how are you doing?' If you need help, go to your father. I am sure he will help you."

Gerald got up from the kitchen table and headed to the garage, where he knew his dad would be. He goes into the garage and sees his dad looking for something. "Hey, Dad, you got a minute?"

"Yeah, son–what do you need?"

"I need some more money," replied Gerald.

"What are you trying to buy now? You got the money for your car, don't you?"

"Yeah, I got the car money, but something came up, and I might be short on getting the car and–" His dad interrupts and asks, "What are you talking about, son? You've gotten yourself into some kind of trouble?"

"No, sir."

"You don't have nobody's daughter pregnant, do you?"

"No, sir."

"Only a woman would have a man talking like you talking. So what's really going on?"

"I was thinking about getting married, Dad."

"Married, are you sure about this? Do you know how much money, time, and energy it will take to get and stay married, Son?"

"Of course, I don't know everything, but we love each other, and we are committed to being together."

"And you are sure about this? How long have you two been dating? A few months?"

"You and Mom met in high school and got married at eighteen. Y'all turned out good."

"Son, that was a different time."

"So you telling me not to get married or you won't help me?"

His dad smirks and puts down the tool in his hand, then takes a seat on a nearby stool. "I know better than to think I can talk you out of this. You are grown. I can't tell you what to do, Gerald. I just would caution you that this is a life decision and will have lasting results. You can't just throw a marriage away when you don't like someone; you have to work it out."

"I know, Dad. I am watching you and Mom. I want what you two have. I know I am young, but we think we can do what y'all did."

"How much money do you need?"

"Like twelve thousand."

"Dang, a few thousand, I would loan it to you, but that kind of money, you are going to have to work for me. I need to make sure I get my money back. I will loan you the money, but you have to enroll in trucking school and agree to work with me for three years."

"Dad, that sounds like slavery," Gerald said as he reacted with a playful grin.

"This is business. I need to be sure you are certain. Anything a man wants, he is willing to work for it. If you aren't willing to do this, you ain't ready to get married and be a husband."

"But Dad, you know I hate trucking. This is your thing, not mine."

"I know, as a man, as a husband, and some-day as a father, you are going to do a lot of things you're not going to like. The funny part is you learn to like it. Do we have a deal?" The two of them did a handshake in the garage, and like that, my dad decided to be a truck driver and get married.

The wedding had the fanfare my mom want-ed. She went over budget, so a ten thousand dollar wedding quickly went to seventeen thousand. My grandfather added two more years to the three to ensure he got his investment back from the wed-ding. Before their wedding, he was nearly done with trucking school and had jobs lined up with his dad.

His job cut down on how many days they could be in Hawaii, not Aruba, and my mom was pissed. On the first day of their honeymoon, while they were sitting on their hotel's balcony the first day. "You are not taking this marriage seriously. If work is going to come first, before me, how is this supposed to work?"

"Kristina, what are you talking about? Do you have any idea how much I have sacrificed to be with you?"

"Oh, so it is a sacrifice to be with me now?

You weren't saying that before. So why are you changing now?"

"Look, I don't know what you're talking about. We have been here for five days. What more do you want?"

"I told you I wanted to be here for two weeks. I think we need to spend time together before we rush back home and you take off driving."

"I told you already, I don't make my schedule."

"Yes, I know, your dad does."

"In this case, he is not my dad; he is my boss. I don't get to dictate or use my affiliation with him for special privileges. I am the newest driver, so I get the worst route to start. It's just the way it is. And I would love to be here with you longer, but I have to start on time to pay for this wedding and some."

"Are we really talking about this again? So, now it is my fault we wanted better food, lights, and a larger reception hall. I told you we could have cut down on the list."

"You wanted me to leave out my cousins while you brought people you barely knew."

"They were the spouses to my family, who I did know."

"Look, I don't want to argue. If that is what is happening, I think we need to go swimming or get something to eat. Maybe we both are a little stressed, so let's go dancing." Gerald gets up, takes Kristina by the hand, and tries to spin her. She gives him a stank stare and says, "I don't feel like going dancing right now, Gerald."

He laughs and says, "Well, I think you may need some space, or I gotta get some fresh air. Call me when you get out of this mood. We are in a tropical paradise, and you want to ride on about stuff that is over and done with. I would like for us to move on so I can enjoy this day of being newly married to my wife. Can we do that?"

She smirked at his statement but didn't respond. He breathes out through his nose and heads to the room. He unpacks his clothes, changes, and re-emerges from the room. "Hey, I am going to head out and get something to eat." Seeing him dressed, she got up from the chair and entered the room. Without a word, she walked past him, close enough to get a whiff of his cologne. He smelt good, tasty, even.

As he waited by the door for her to say, "Bye," she came from the room dressed in heels and poppin' lipstick number eight from BWC Cosmetics, which made him remember why he married her. She walked up to the door and said, "I'm ready. Where are we going to eat?"

My mom was always sassy and demanding. My dad liked it in the beginning. He thought it meant she was jealous over him, but he missed that she could have actually been more controlling. My mom wanted what she wanted at that moment, and if she didn't get her way, she was quick to stomp her feet and start withdrawing.

I never wanted to be like her in that sense, using my emotions to weaponize my feelings to penalize and guilt trip people into doing things they might not want to do. Did my dad really love my mom, or did he just not want to see her with someone else? Did he allow his worries to trigger a response that honestly could have waited more months or years to be made?

If they both hadn't had their own agendas, perhaps I would have been born into a marriage that would have lasted.

My parents had a typical marriage that lasted less than two years. As you can see, day one was a challenge, and the months to come would prove just as difficult. With the honeymoon ending quickly and life kicking in, they both were not ready for what life would bring. When my mom and dad got off the plane and entered the car to head home, they went to an apartment that didn't have lights cut on yet.

When my mom opened the door, the first thing she asked was, "Where are the lights at?" Her nose turned up as if she smelled days-old garbage. My dad replied, "I am not sure what's going on. I called my order in before we left. It should be on."

She smirks and smacks her lips. She assumed he had forgotten, but moments later, he was told that he had made the request, and it was an honest oversight. The power company apologized and said they would be out later that day or tomorrow morning at the latest.

He tried to joke and kid and said, "Maybe we should have a candlelight dinner to set the mood?" Kristina replied, "Or we could go out to eat and pray the lights are on when we come back. We can't move anything in the dark, Gerald."

He replied, "You sure have a way with words, Beautiful."

"Yes, it is called honesty," replied Kristina.

"Or is it a little bit of cruelty?" Gerald asked with a playful smirk.

"What you trying to say?"

"That I want us to enjoy this day and not allow lights to be the reason we miss this moment. We are in our own place that we paid for. It is not perfect, but it is ours. I am proud of us." He walks into the kitchen, opens the door, and says, "Look here, we got a fridge!" He turns on the kitchen sink and says, "Running water, and at least we can take a shower," he says as he tries to cuddle with her in the kitchen.

"So you want me to risk getting my hair wet in a cold shower and not be able to blow dry my hair? I am going to look like Frankenstein's wife." Gerald laughed and said, "But you are my wife. I love you with wild hair, your hair, or however you come. And I can think of a couple of reasons you will need a cold shower." She giggles and says, "Okay, I just might take you up on that offer." She comes close and kisses him, and just like God, the power comes on.

"Yes, let's look at the positive, Babe. Secondly, let's try out that shower." The two of them giggle while walking to their room. They enter, and the door gently shuts behind them. All the moments weren't bad. It's just so sad that the happy moments didn't outweigh the good. My dad would head to work the next day feeling like a million bucks.

He wasn't just going to work; he was going to work for his family! He had a little wife at home who loved him, and he was willing to work for her to be happy and to be provided for. Going to work now seemed more important. He wanted to show up for his wife first and then his dad. He never wanted to get behind a truck until that day.

He entered the office with a smile. His dad looked him over with a matching smile and said, "Are you ready, Son?"

"I'm good."

"Ready to take your driving test?"

"Yeah, I think I am good to take the test."

"How was the honeymoon?"

"It was good. It started off a little bumpy, if I am honest."

"That's normal. I remember your mom and I getting into a little fight that ended quickly. It is a good sign. So, don't be alarmed."

"That's good to hear. We've been pretty good since. I am excited to get to work, though."

"Yeah, a wife can make you push harder, and a baby will make you break your neck to survive and see them good. So far, I am proud of you son."

"Thanks, Dad. That means a lot." They both head out of his dad's office to greet the team. His dad officially introduces him to the team and lets them know that if his test goes well this week, he will be taken on John's route. John is beyond thrilled to start training Gerald the following week. He has been praying to get rid of this shift since he started. His wife has been complaining about him never being home, especially because they have a newborn on the way.

"Alright, don't get too excited. He still has to take the test, and although I believe he is ready, I don't want us to jinx it."

John replies, "You know anybody close to you can drive. I am sure he is passing with flying colors. I am going to let my wife know, yall don't know how much this means, for real." My dad didn't say much, but he was paying attention. One thing about my dad, he doesn't talk much but listens to what people are saying. At that moment, he knew he would have to work to keep his marriage tight.

He went to Google to see what he could do because he wasn't sure what wives liked. Girlfriends expected stuff on holidays, her birthday, and special occasions, but wives wanted things just because! He didn't have the luxury of what other men could learn about their wives by spending time with them. Being over the road meant being away from home, so he missed out on that.

He took the test and passed it as projected; he would start training for his route the following week. He was elated and exhausted on the first few nights of being away from home. He didn't realize being away from home would impact him as much as it did. Although he had only been married for a few weeks, it was hard to leave her. He hated saying goodbye on Monday, knowing it wouldn't be until late Wednesday night that he would see her again.

He wanted this week to be special, so he got home with flowers, only to find that his wife had been long asleep. He tiptoed into the shower and cleaned up since it had been hours since the last rest stop. He wanted to see her up to greet him, but she looked so peaceful sleeping. He watched her rest and loved that she was safe in their house.

For several months, they went on like this, him working and coming home to his sleeping beauty. It didn't bother him until life for his wife changed. She was fresh out of high school and still looking for herself. She wasn't sure what she wanted to do, but having a husband who paid the bills gave her time to think. She appreciated the time she had to figure out her thoughts and life, but she was still stuck on what direction to pursue.

She considered majoring in business, but after seeing what they made and the hours, time, and money spent on college, she decided against it. She didn't want to be in school forever. She honestly wanted a quick fix to a problem: independence. She was raised in a stable home with both parents and siblings before they died in a car accident. She wanted that, and she was building it. But she couldn't help but remember how she wished to be free.

She wondered why she felt the way she did about being free when her husband was out the door more than he was home. If she was honest, she loved him but liked being home alone more without him than with him. It was concerning, but she buried the thought. She wasn't sure where that feeling came from and assumed it would fade.

As she searched the internet for growing fields, she stumbled upon Melvina Washington. She had a convincing and powerful way of talking about medical coding, a field Kristina had never even heard of. She knew there was medical billing but didn't really know what coders do. After binge-watching several reels, she felt like an expert in the industry and wanted in!

She wanted to register for class, but only she had no money to pay for it. Gerald had a bank account before the two of them married, and he wasn't too transparent about how much he had. They never talked about money, and he usually gave her cash for the bills. She didn't have to give an account of what was spent, but it made her feel uneasy to know that she had to ask him for money to do something she wanted to do for herself.

So, she thought she would get a part-time job. She called her husband while he was driving, and as usual, he was happy to hear from her. The two of them talked often because she was home, and he was on the open road. Many nights, she talked him to the next dropoff when he thought he wouldn't make it, and he was grateful for her.

"Hey, Babe, what's up?"

"Doing good, just thinking," replies Kristina.

"Oh yeah, about what?"

"About getting a job."

"Okay, so you want to get a job in what field?"

"I don't know yet. I just thought it would be good to get a job."

"Yeah, I can see you wanting to get out of the house. That's cool."

"Well, I will need a few things to get started."

"Well, I will drop you some more money so you can do what you need to." Gerald didn't need a hint. He knew his wife would want to do some things for herself, and he never wanted her to feel like a caged bird. He would miss talking to her at all times of the night because he knew her working meant him sharing her time with others.

He gave her $500, which was plenty of money to get her hair and nails done and buy some outfits for wherever she would work. She thought to get something in the office even though she lacked experience. She went on job sites and started filling out applications. She filled out ten applications a day. After seven days of this, she thought, why wasn't anyone calling?

Was it what she wrote? Did her lack of experience scare people away? So, she thought of embellishing her resume a bit and claiming skills that she had started researching on websites, video platforms, and social media. She was growing in confidence but wasn't fully prepared for the callback she would receive in two short days.

The caller said, "Hi, this is Jasmine from R&R Construction. Is this Kristina?" She quickly replied, "Yes, this is she." The caller said that she would like to have her come in for an interview or do a video conference to interview her as quickly as possible. Kristina was ready and agreed to meet that same week. Jasmine and my mom got on well real quick. So good that Jasmine gave her the job on the spot, and they started hanging out later that weekend.

My mom loved the company, but in hindsight, Jasmine might not have been the ideal friend for my mother. Jasmine was single and loved being single for all the liberties it gave her. She had no intention of getting married anytime soon. She made that clear every chance she got. She found a way to take a jab at my mother's marriage every chance she got.

One day, while the two of them were watching a movie and hanging out at my mom's, she asked, "What's the point of being married if he is never home?"

"It's not like that, Jasmine. He drives trucks."

"I don't care if he rode airplanes. He should make you a priority and be home more. Girl, you don't know what he is doing out there on that road."

"Don't go there. I know my husband, and he ain't looking for nobody else," replied Kristina.

"And what makes you so sure? Men are not loyal but only as faithful as their options," replied Jasmine. She went on to say, "How old are you anyway? Twenty-two or twenty-three?"

"Twenty," replied Kristina.

"Girl, you sure you weren't a statutory rape victim or something? Why in the hell did you get married so young? You do know you have a whole life to live. Why would you get married so early?"

"Because I love him."

"Love, you barely had anybody. Is he your first?"

"Yes, but I don't see what that has to do with this."

"So you are okay with dying, knowing you only had one?"

"One, what? Relationship?"

"Girl, you are so green. Nah, I mean–"

"Oh, girl, you nasty."

"Naw, I am real. Don't tell me you have never thought of someone else other than your husband?"

"No, it's only been him," replied Kristina.

"Well then, you are a goody-toe shoe. I can tell you, ain't no way I would be satisfied with only one. I am not telling you to go out here and slut yourself out, but one, that's wasting your youth. You are a pretty girl with your whole life ahead of you. You ain't got no kids, and you can do what you want to do. I think we should go out tonight."

"Girl, I don't go to clubs. I am more of a Netflix and chill kind of person."

"That's why you are married. You're boring."

"Boring? I'm not boring."

"Okay, let me guess, you go bowling, eat at restaurants, you might read a book or two, and you are thinking about going to school to fill your time. Am I right? Predictable and boring!"

"So what are you doing?"

"I just came back from Mexico on a girl's trip. We went out there and cut up. I had so much fun. I plan on going to Vegas next month and a cruise for my birthday. Girl, I am living my best life because we ain't young forever. You better use this time to enjoy yourself. Don't saddlebag yourself to a relationship or a man. You gonna be here cooking and cleaning with a baby on the way feeling stuck."

"Stuck?"

"Yes, stuck. You are going to be Susie Homemaker, staying at home with three or four kids, having a boring life, and having a boring husband. I assume he does what you do?" Jasmine started laughing, but realizing Kristina got quiet, she gently said, "Hey, why don't we go out and just hang out?

"A few weeks ago, we came back from Hawaii, thank you. And I enjoy my life. Yes, we spend a lot of time at home, but it works for us."

"I am not trying to change you, Kristina. I just want you to live a little. You can be you, of course, and if this makes you happy, cool."

"Okay, cool. "

"But I still do think we should go out. Just once. If you don't like it, we can leave. Will you go out with me, please, please?" My mom hated the tables being turned on her. She couldn't refuse Jasmine's puppy eyes, so she agreed to go.

Getting dressed wasn't difficult because my mom loved clothes. She didn't realize she hadn't gone into her closet to grab more than a pair of sweatpants in the last few months. Her birthday was coming up, and she didn't know what she wanted to do.

When dressed, Jasmine looked at her and said, "I see you, Boo. Let me find out you had a good time wrapped up like a pig in a blanket." The two started laughing and called their ride. Neither one of them felt like driving downtown on the weekend. Kristina knew her husband would be calling, so she pretended to be sleepy and got off the phone quickly. After saying, "I love you too," she snuck off.

Standing in line, she didn't think too much about who might see her. It wasn't until she saw a familiar car that she was alerted to the dangers of being seen by her in-laws. She knew her grandmother had never left the house, so no worries there.

For a second, she stood with her back toward the street until she thought, why would they be out at this hour anyway? She was sure they were at home sleeping like she would be normally. She loved her quiet life, and tonight was to shut up Jasmine and keep her from thinking she was boring.

She got to the top of the line, and the guard asked, "Ladies IDs?"

Jasmine reached into her small clutch saddle strapped across her body for their IDs. He scanned the IDs, gave Kristina a wristband, and said, "Okay, y'all ladies, have a good night." They enter the club, and the music is bumping.

Jasmine seemed to be right at home as she was touched by the music booming from the speakers. Her head started bobbing as she walked the floor, and Kristina played it cool. She was into rap music, of course, but she didn't headbang to it; it was more like listening to it when scanning social media posts.

Jasmine taps her and says, "Let's get a drink." Kristina nods and follows behind her while she dances her way to the bar. She got to the bartender and asked, "Can I have a rum and pineapple juice?" She ordered like a regular, and the bartender looked at her and gave her a friendly smile. Then, seeing my mom's wristband, he offered her bottled water or soda.

Kristina got water because she wasn't big on soda. She wasn't extremely health conscious, but she hated acne. Her face would break out terribly when she drank soda, so she gave it up years back.

The ladies went to the dance floor and bounced around for several songs. They didn't have to say a word, as if they could hear it with the music blasting and vibration radiating from the floor. They kidded and played around until a man with braids and a big smile came up behind Jasmine.

He whispered in her ear, and she grinned. She didn't look behind her but kept on dancing. Kristina took that as her cue to escape to the bathroom. After drinking that water, she was dying to pee.

Leaving the bathroom and entering the main floor, she looked for Jasmine. As she scanned the room, she was unaware of glaring eyes locked in on her location. She moved toward the floor, and a gentle hand grab for hers. He brought her close to him to speak into her ear, "Hey, you looking for somebody?" She replies, "Yeah, I am trying to find my friend. She's here somewhere."

"Oh, I can help you find her. What is she wearing?" Kristina described her to him, and the two of them were off on a mission. As they searched the club, they couldn't find her anywhere. She thought she might have gone outside, so she went near the door, and she called her name, "Jasmine."

Outside the club, she walked in both directions, but she still didn't see her. It was a bit awkward now to be walking with this stranger outside the club. She thought of thanking him and dismissing him to head home. But at that moment, he offered to take her home, and she replied, "No thanks. I'm good. I got a ride out here, so I can just call to get home."

"Then, do you mind if I get your number?"

She replied, "Oh, sorry, I am married."

"Okay, congratulations. We can be friends. No pressure."

"Naw, I don't think that is a good idea."

"Okay, I'm here sometimes. Maybe next time, we can link up and look for your friend again then? Oh, what's your name?"

"Kristina."

"Okay, I'm Javier. Nice to meet you. You sure you don't want me to wait for your car or help you check one more time for your friend?"

"No, I can just give her a call." Kristina started patting her outfit and remembered she had given Jasmine her phone and ID to carry in her purse. "Dang it."

"What?"

"I don't have my phone. Jasmine has it."

"It's cool. I can call the ride for you. I mean–if you comfortable with that?"

"Thank you, I appreciate that. I am going to kill her when I see her tomorrow."

"Yeah, it's all good." He got her address and called her ride. He stayed and waited around with her. As the two of them chatted, Kristina was sure to keep her distance. She didn't notice inside the club, but Javier was very good-looking. He had light eyes, wore braids, and had what many would say was good hair.

Not a moment too soon, the car pulled up, and she thanked him again. She offered to send him money for the ride, but he said, "Don't worry about it. I just want to see you get home safe." She thanked him, and she was off. With no numbers exchanged, she felt good about her outing, but honestly, she had no intentions of going out again.

Jasmine didn't come to her house until the next morning, around 6 a.m., to bring her phone and ID. Kristina tried to hold her peace and said, "Where did you go last night? You left me stranded with no ID, phone, or money."

"My bad, I was there at the club. I didn't leave. I was just in the parking lot. We walked out the front, and when I came back to look for you, you were gone."

"Okay, so why didn't you meet me back here?"

"I didn't get a ride home; the guy I met drove me."

"Really, you left with that guy?"

"Yes, don't judge me, this isn't an inquisition. I am grown."

"I'm not going to ask any more questions, but where is my stuff?"

"Dang, you ain't going to invite me in?"

"Right now, no!"

"Come on, don't be like that. Be honest, we had fun."

"It started out that way until I got ditched, stranded, and had to ask for help to get home. It was embarrassing, honestly."

"Hey, you got home, right?" replied Jasmine as she gave Kristina her stuff.

"Okay, thank you, and goodbye, Jasmine."
As she closed the door, Jasmine replied, "Come on, Kristina. Don't be like that. I really apologize for last night. It will never happen again."

"You right, because I ain't going out with you no more."

"Why, I am fun."

"No, you are a ghost."

She laughs and says, "Can I come in? I really gotta pee?" Kristina, against her better judgment, opens the door. Jasmine storms into the bathroom. Kristina's phone rings, and her husband is on the line. She didn't want to explain why Jasmine was at her house at the crack of dawn, so she purposely missed the call. Jasmine emerges from the bathroom, and she asks, "Are you good now?"

"Dang–why you sound like you want me to leave or something?"

"Because I am tired, and I need more rest. I am not used to staying out all night."

"Yeah, it gets easier. I am still working tomorrow, even if I am hungover. Staying out doesn't bother me. I just need a quick nap to refuel."

"This isn't going to be a habit for me."

"Jasmine plops down on the couch and says, "Kristina, dame, would you please live a little? Hanging out with me will bring some fun to your life. That's probably why God had you and I meet."

She hits Jasmine with a pillow, and the two start laughing and talking about Jasmine's wild night. When her husband called her later that morning, it was an awkward conversation, and Kristina wasn't sure why. Was she still thinking about the guy with the braids? Could Jasmine be right about needing more experience? Was she missing out on life by marrying young?

Kristina pushed past the thoughts and focused on starting her job on Monday! She was thrilled to start living her life. She did feel like she was missing out on life, being cooped up in the house all day, waiting for her husband to return. It was a weird Rapunzel vibe that she couldn't pinpoint, but she wanted out of the tower.

She enjoyed going to work and having a sense of purpose. She was committed to doing this job to work for enough money to finish medical coding school. She only needed about $1,500.

When she started working, she realized that with her money, she could do what she wanted. This quick job (gotten to help her afford school) could afford whatever she wanted to buy. Life was beginning to feel good, but she felt off. She wasn't sure if it was the hours because she was quick to come in for someone else's shift. She was saving to buy a purse she knew her husband would say no to her having.

Lately, his number one focus was paying off his dad, and she low-key hated it. He didn't budget spending more than what he said they could afford for anything. On the one hand, she liked that he was responsible, but she loathed that he was ridged. She wanted him to relax and budge a little so they could have fun, but he would explain why they needed to do things his way to pay for what was owed.

She got tired of talking to him and decided she would do it herself when he was gone. Every weekend, she went to different places to buy what she wanted. He didn't bother asking her what she was doing with her money because he knew he was tight-fisted with funds. He commended her for getting her own money, given that she wanted to splurge on expensive shoes and purses he saw hanging up in the closet or that came out unmentioned during date night.

He would say she looked nice but knew she was changing under his nose. Something was different, and he couldn't tell what it was. That was until one night, while out to eat, she excused herself from the table and took three steps before she barfed all over the floor. The waiters assured her it wasn't a problem, but she felt so embarrassed that she wanted to leave immediately. They tipped the waiter for what they had and left.

The ride home was filled with my dad's concerns and my mom asking him to pull over a few times. She had to ride with the car window down and her head out the window to cool off. She was very hot and seemed to be running a fever.

When they got home, she headed for the

bathroom before lying down. She said she was hungry but couldn't bring herself to eat a bite. Gerald was concerned and suggested she go to urgent care. She told him she was fine and just needed some rest. She thought she could have gotten food poisoning, and it just needed to pass.

The next day, she got up and felt like death was knocking at her door. She felt so sick she didn't want to get out of bed. Gerald, concerned, called in to work and took his wife to the hospital. They ran several tests and asked if she might be pregnant. She hadn't thought about pregnancy because it hadn't come up. Moments after the test was taken, the nurse popped up and said with a big smile, "All this fuss is likely about the baby."

Gerald blinks slowly and intentionally and says, "Sorry, what?"

"Yeah, your wife is pregnant. Congratulations." Kristina is still speechless. She heard the nurse, but she was still dazed. A part of her would have wanted to know this privately, but she did say they could be open about her results. She wanted her husband to know if something was wrong—it was his fault if she had an infection. She never thought she would be pregnant.

She started thinking long, quick, and fast. My dad spoke to the nurse about the next steps, and she suggested they follow up with an OBGYN. It took my mom longer to know how she felt, and although Gerald was encouraging, she was nervous. How will this baby change her life? Will she now have to buy baby stuff with her money?

She knew it was selfish to think of the purses and shoes she would have to put on hold because of a baby, but those were things she really wanted, and she was willing to work for them. She was saving for that purse, and now, it seemed further away. Going to school also seemed to be pushed further down the road with the baby coming. She wasn't happy, but she was also not sad. She was in this weird gray space.

If she had prayed, she might have prayed about it, but religion was never something she practiced. Sure, she knew there was a God who didn't know that, but she never thought of talking to Him. She saw too many lives that looked like God moved too slowly for her liking. Having nine months to get ready for the baby was not a time span she wanted to speed up.

She was married and financially secure, but if she was honest, she didn't want a baby right now. If she knew a way to bring up the conversion, she would have asked her husband for an abortion. It just didn't seem like the right thing to do with both families so excited about their first grandbaby. The pressure was overwhelming.

She suffered in silence and said nothing. She came up with an excuse for the purse being a push gift. Because she had a will, she was also determined to make a way. If only the rest of her life could have been so simple.

She had to find a way to get what she wanted, even though I, the interloper, was crashing the party. I don't think she was ever connected to me during her pregnancy. Maybe she struggled to balance the things she wanted for herself with what my dad would make a priority for me. It would be hard to picture a mother jealous of her own child, but some fingers could point there.

She knew she had six more months to go before I arrived, and because she started her appointments late in her pregnancy, the remaining doctor's appointments would fly by. That might have been a kiss from Yah to her.

Getting pregnant seemed to come at a terrible time. She was just finding her groove at work, and now she can't sit still for longer than an hour before running to the bathroom. The constant breaks annoyed her so much.

Before she had confirmation of her pregnancy, she had practically no signs of being pregnant. The moment it was confirmed, morning sickness kicked in with a vengeance. People in the office started to tell her that her mommy glow was kicking in.

Ironically, although she had a mommy glow, she was also being told she was having a girl because her beauty faded. How does your beauty fade anyway? She thought she looked the same, and her weight didn't pile on, so what were they seeing? How was I pulling beauty if she looked the same—she didn't even have a watermelon in the front yet? It wasn't until the physical changes started to kick in that Kristina realized how much she did not like being pregnant.

She vowed never to get pregnant again—one was enough, and she was officially a one-and-done chick. Gerald was ecstatic to see her belly growing with his baby. He was buying things and bringing more gifts back for the baby than he ever did for his wife. He was in love with the baby he had not met yet. Kristina would try to calm him down and keep him to a budget, but he would splurge–in his way–and bring back new things all the time.

If I didn't know any better, I would say my mom was not jealous of another woman stealing her husband's heart but the baby. She started to feel like a incubator carrying his baby and not his wife. She didn't realize how much she had begun to drift away from him.

The love she thought she had for him felt less and less like love. Having me didn't bring them closer at all. Not to say I was the reason for the break. They were boycotting sex long before I was visible. But my mom hated her pregnant body. She wanted to slim down long before giving birth. She knew she was pregnant, but that didn't stop her from grinding and looking at the scale. She didn't have that cute journey of being pregnant and wanting to make a cast of her belly.

She wanted the belly off and the baby out! I am not sure if I made her hate motherhood or if, honestly, she should have never been a mother. I know it is not my place to suggest this, being I wouldn't be here without her. I guess I learned to understand my mom, but when I got real about what she wanted, I was forced to realize that that wasn't me.

Whenever I think to take it personally, I stop. We cannot help the way another person feels. We can only seek to understand the person. The day I was born was an eventful one. You would have thought music would fill the room and joy. I cannot say it was rainbows, hearts, and butterflies, however. My mom and dad found out I was a girl when she was twenty weeks along. My dad was grateful, but I think my mom might have wanted a son. Having two girls in my dad's life just made her so uptight. I don't know why she hated me so much when she didn't even know me yet.

It could have been the money my dad spent that she felt should have been spent spoiling her. I think she grew resentful that the things he wouldn't do for her, he did for me without me ever asking. It makes you wonder how she got this kind of mindset as a mother.

She was selfish, and even on my day of birth, she only could think of her needs. She got an epidural to help push me out. I know that she was in labor for twenty-eight hours with me. Her water broke, and the process snailed along. She tried going to the hospital and was only two and a half centimeters dilated. So, they sent her home and told her to come back when the pain became unbearable, and her contractions were about five minutes apart. They wouldn't admit my mom if she were less than four centimeters dilated.

She looked up everything she could do to speed up the process. She tried spicy foods, castor oil, pineapples, and red-leaf tea, but nothing seemed to push her along. It was as if I was waiting for my dad to arrive. My dad was on the road when I broke her water. I came two weeks earlier than expected, so my dad was over the road.

He didn't want to miss me being born even though he said he might faint. My mom laughed at first, but then, she had no comment. She became silent as the weeks went along. My dad also embraced the empty space as he became uncertain about what to do. He thought the depression could have been from her having a baby when their relationship was rocky. She was in a low place, he knew, but he knew nothing about how to support her.

He just thought she was selfish and tried to convince her that she was not alone. His mom planned to help my mom take care of me, and she recognized the issue, which no one else knew enough to diagnose. She suggested my mom speak with someone, but my mom politely told her to mind her own business. She didn't say it matter-of-factly, but she never called the numbers her mother-in-law gave to her. She even threw the paper in the trash. She thought the idea of speaking to someone was stupid because it couldn't change her circumstances.

She didn't want this baby but was being made to have it. She was past her time of return, and now she was on the hook for bringing a life into the world. This baby was stretching her body, costing money that could have been hers, and taking her beauty all at the same time. She was miserable going upstairs and walking around the office in the later weeks. As she walked the block for what seemed like three hours, her contractions started to get closer.

She wanted to shower and freshen up before heading to the hospital. Only, while in the tub, she slipped on the slick tiles and bumped her head. She wasn't sure for how long she was out, but her contractions were closer than before. She was only woken up because the pain became too powerful for her to sleep through. She woke up knowing she was in labor.

She had dry blood on her forehead that she thought to cover with her hair. She couldn't stand long enough to clean it all out before another pain would come, shifting her focus. She did her best and put on the quickest dress she could find. The dress was almost too short, but she didn't care. Soon, I would be out, and the dress would be a perfect fit!

She knew better than to drive herself to the

hospital, so she called her grandmother. But her grandmother (affectionately known as her mom) didn't pick up. Now, she had no other choice but to call her mother-in-law. It seemed like she was on speed dial because she was at my mother's house in fifteen minutes. The drive was normally twenty minutes or more, so she knew she had been speeding.

She arrived back at the hospital, and this time, she knew her labor had intensified. She felt a bit dizzy from her fall, but the pain had her push that aside to focus on the matter at hand: delivering a baby.

Her husband had called her several times, but she didn't catch his calls. Lately, it wasn't uncommon for them to miss each other's calls. The way she felt right then, she wasn't sure if it was good he was there or not. Surprisingly, he arrived three hours later, two hours before my mom pushed me out.

He was excited to be there and was very accommodating. Although my mom was taking her frustrations out on the people in the room, they were all accommodating and didn't complain. They didn't care that she was ignoring their comments and small talk, and she shh'd them a few times when she wasn't the center of attention. Just when they were going to exit the room to allow her to sleep a bit and get something to drink, Kristina let out a loud cry.

Uncertain of the cause, Gerald was back at her bedside, asking her if everything was alright. "No, I am having a baby. I am in pain."

"Okay, like, is this baby pain, back pain? Do you think you need to push?"

"How am I supposed to know Gerald? I am not the doctor."

"Of course, I can get the nurse for you."

"No, I have the remote right here. I will just push the button."

"Is there anything I can do?"

"No, you can just stand there and watch me in pain."

"Aww, boo, I wish I could help you more. I really do. Can I get you some ice or something?"

"No, I want you to be here. You can't feel what I am feeling, but at least be here."

"Okay, I will be right here." His mom overhears the conversation because Kristina is not whispering, and she exits the room to go get coffee. She hasn't said a negative word to Kristina, but if she could speak at that moment, she would have said nothing and probably just slapped her for being so selfish. She hated when women took advantage of her son, and she felt that that was what Kristina was doing.

My mom acted as if she didn't want him around until he was leaving. I guess her desire not to be alone was stronger than her disdain for him at the moment. My mom kept saying snappy things that my grandmother could not stand, but the ultimate wrong was when she dismissed my grandmother from the room! My dad tried to comfort the women and bring down the emotions, but Kristina only got louder. To keep order, his mother left and wished him the best of luck.

It broke her heart to leave, but it also frustrated Gerald. Kristina was being extremely selfish. Her emotional rollercoaster made her vitals go crazy, stressing me out, and, to make matters worse, she argued more. He could only keep his peace as his mother walked out, and Cruela lay in the bed, blowing smoke from her nostrils.

It would be another hour before she would give birth. When the doctor came in and said, "Alright, we are ready. I want you to give me a big push." She pushed, gripping the hands of her husband and the bed. As she followed doctors' orders to push several more times, she was relieved when the doctor said, "She's out."

Shortly after, I was rushed to the nurses' table, where they wiped me off and pricked my foot. I didn't make a sound until they pricked me, and it was extremely brief. If I had not been born with my eyes open and looking around, you would have thought I was asleep.

My dad seemed to have floated over to me and dropped my mom's hand to grab mine. The nurse placed me in his arms, and he was crying as he held me. He thought no woman would have him wrapped around her finger so quickly, but I was the one who best my mother. My mother was still delivering the afterbirth while she watched the father-daughter moment.

She never told me how she felt watching my dad marvel at me. I can only imagine that she felt jealous because of the events that followed. You would never think a mother would envy a father's relationship with his daughter, but somehow she did. My dad was committed to staying in the hospital the entire time I was there.

He watched from the glass with a big smile on his face. The nurses admired him so much that one of the nurses offered him the chance to bathe me, and without hesitation, he did it. My first hug and bath by either parent was by my dad. When

I was washed and bundled up, I was given to my mother because she said, "Can you clean her off first? I don't want the white stuff on me."

She held me in her arms, but I don't think she felt the magic my dad did. She saw me, yet the instinctual bond a mother has with her baby was never felt with me. She just stared at me. It was like I felt the rejection, and I started to cry. The nurses indicated that I was hungry and that she should try to breastfeed me. She replied, "Oh, I don't want to breastfeed."

The nurse said, "We can send in a lactation specialist if you like–to show you how. You don't have to be nervous."

"I said I am not breastfeeding this baby. What didn't you understand?"

"Yes, ma'am, I will go and get you a bottle."

My father said, "Thanks so much, I really appreciate it." He looks at his wife, whose breasts are tingling. He says to her, "Boo, I can help. You want me to get her?" I can call my mom back in if you want someone to talk to about this."

"No, Gerald. I want people to hear me. I don't want to breastfeed."

"Okay, you have been through a lot. So you don't have to try now. It's okay."

"No, I don't want to do this period."

"Okay, it's just breastfeeding is the best thing for the baby." As Kristina continues to hold me, my cries grow louder. She replied in a frustrated tone, "Here you come and get the baby. She clearly likes you more, and I am tired."

"Aww, don't feel like that. She's just hungry. I know she loves you. Do you want to feed the baby when the nurse gets back?" He took me from her arms and she grunted, and turned her back to him. He started to rock me and sing a melody that calmed my nerves. I don't know how my dad became the baby whisperer, but since that day, he just knew how to help me calm down.

When the nurse returned with the bottles, she explained her recommended feeding schedule and how to burp me when I was done. She offered to come back and check on him to be sure he was comfortable burping me. He was nervous about patting me too hard.

That day, my dad's heart was filled with so much more joy. He always calls me "Joy," even though my mother named me Kimberly. She wanted a name that was similar to hers and different. My dad agreed to what she picked, and two days later, we were all discharged from the hospital.

Getting home was challenging. My mom didn't know what to do, and my father did most of the feeding, diaper changes, and helping me sleep. My mother stayed in the room and rested. She had no complications with the birth, but you would have thought she delivered a village with how much she felt drained each day. My dad begged my grandmother to come and help her. With much fuss, she agreed.

As my dad was leaving to get back to work, he told his mother, "Mom, I really do appreciate you being here."

"Son, I am here for you and my grandbaby."

"I know Kristina is going through a tough time. But you are a wonderful mother, and I think she can learn some things from you. She doesn't have a mother, so we both have to be patient."

"You are right, Son. I will do my best." Gerald gives the baby to his mom right after he kisses her goodbye. My grandmother loved holding me and singing. I think my dad got that from her because she always sang to me, too. You would have thought my mom was grateful for my grandmother's presence, but she only burned more with envy.

If she saw me happy with someone else, she questioned why not her. But when she held me, she didn't want to. My grandmother sat her down one day and said, "I think you should talk to someone, Kristina."

"About what, Mom?"

"I think you have postpartum depression."

"Really, you think I need to see a therapist?"

"I am just saying I know it can be tough having a new baby with all the changes. Sometimes, we may need some help to adjust."

"Did you need some help to adjust to having your children?"

"No, but every woman is different."

"Exactly, there is nothing wrong with me. I am a different mother than you."

"I can respect that; it is just that I see you have changed, and I am…concerned."

"Life has a way of changing everybody, Momma. We can't stay the same when life keeps going ahead."

"Alright, I see we are going to disagree. Do you need me to do anything else before I head out?"

"You are leaving early. Don't you want to stay a bit longer?"

"Actually, I have a date with my husband, and I can't. But I am sure you and the baby will be fine. If you need something that is an emergency, call me or 911."

She gets up, grabs her purse, and heads out the door. As soon as the door shut, it was as if I knew love had exited the room and woke up crying. "Aw, come on! What is wrong now? I just got a moment of peace, and here she goes, already." She sits several minutes more before she gets up to check on me. She enters the room and sees that I kicked out of being bundled up.

She reached into the crib and picked me up. She brought me close, and I rested on her chest. Hearing her heartbeat, I kicked less. She wrapped her arms underneath my butt and rocked me like she saw others do. She started singing but stopped and patted me gently on the back. I drifted back off to sleep.

Chapter 5

The following days were challenging for my mother because she and my grandmother got into a few disagreements. My mom wanted things to be her way even though she wasn't sure of what that looked like. It didn't stop her from telling my grandmother how she felt. She wasn't sure if my father's absence made her on edge, but she was like a raging bull in a china shop when it came to simple topics. She was defensive and cold.

One day, after telling my grandmother to leave, she broke down and called Jasmine. She said on the phone, "Jasmine, hey, how are you doing?"

"Great girl. I am out and about, getting stuff done. I've been meaning to come by and see you and the baby. I've just been busy."

"Oh, it's okay. I know you still have a life."

"Of course I do. I warned you how much life can change when a baby comes. Am I right, or am I right? You're probably in that house going crazy and snapping at everybody, ain't you?"

"No comment."

"Enough said. So why are you really calling me?"

"I need you to come over. Please!" she said, emphasizing the "z" sound in please. Jasmine did a joking scoff and said, "I ain't holding no baby. And I ain't burping her, either. Babies throw up like in the exorcist."

"I know a few other things to add to the list. I just could use some company. With someone that isn't demanding."

"Oh girl, you might want to call someone else then. I am always asking for something."

"Well, you have legs to get it yourself. How about that?"

"Touché." The ladies hang up, and Kristina stares at the wall. She is pondering how she got here and what she is doing. I am not even twenty-one and already married with a baby, stuck at home, and feeling extra stuck! She wanted out and didn't know how to get out–or even why she wanted out so badly.

The minutes passed while she waited on Jasmine's snail's pace. My mom heard me crying in the background, but she didn't feel moved to get up. She was stuck, and she felt bad, but she needed a break. She had to get out, but where would she go?

Jasmine rang the bell. Kristina quickly rose from her seat. She jogged to the door and opened it to see Jasmine on her phone speaking with someone. "Hey!" replied Kristina. A bit startled to see her appear so quickly, Jasmine says, "Well, dang, did you fly to the door? How are you doing? And is your baby crying, or is that the tv?"

"Oh, that's the baby; I will go get her in a minute. I ain't trying to spoil her by picking her up all the time." Jasmine raises an eyebrow and walks into the house as Kristian practically drags her inside. "Girl, you need to go get that baby. She is loud, and I don't see how you can do anything but tend to yo baby. I can wait right here." Jasmine starts to move toward the door, but Kristina pulls her back gently.

"Please, don't leave me." Jasmine, seeing her face, knew she needed to focus and get off the phone. She responded to the person on the other end, "Hey, I gotta let you go. My friend needs my help. Okay, I'll call you back. Bye."

Jasmine looks at Kristina and says, "You know my rules. What can I do to help?" Jasmine walks with her to my room. At this point, I had been crying for nearly twenty-five minutes. The ladies walk into the room, and Jasmine is pulled to look into the crib to see what tiny body is making all this noise. As she looks in, the baby is still wiggling and crying.

She reaches for the baby and picks her up; only the back of the baby is soaked. She had a blowout, and the smell was horrid. Jasmine says, "Uhun, this baby stank. You need to get your child and change her. She has poop all down her back. I would be crying, too!" She pushes the baby in front of Kristina.

Kristina pushes her back toward her gently and says, "I am sure she just did that. I swear she does that daily. Do you mind helping me?"

"Now, I told you I don't do poop, Kristina. Get yo, baby." Jasmine pushes me back in her direction.

"I know, but I am really struggling here. She has been awake and sleeping, crying off and on all day. I am tired. I need to do my hair and nails and just have a me day. I really can't do this, Jasmine."

"Okay, I am only helping you this one time. Don't think I am going to be coming here to change your baby's poopy diapers." Jasmine brings the baby to the changing table. She starts to unclothe the baby and asks Kristina for a pacifier to help soothe the baby. The baby was no longer kicking and screaming, and Jasmine was trying to keep herself from grossing out. She yelled to Kristina, "Girl, get a trash bag so I can get rid of this."

"You throwing away the clothes, Jasmine?" She snaps around and looks at Kristina, "What, you are going to clean this and use it again? Girl, this is ruined and will never be the same. You might as well throw this away now and save your nose from the smells."

Kristina obliges and throws it into the waste basket near Jasmine's feet. After I am all clean, she offers me up, but Kristina turns away and says, "You mind feeding her for me?" as she gives her a prepared bottle.

"Come on, Kristina!"

"This isn't burping her; I just need you to feed her. She is quiet now, so she likes you." Jasmine smacks her lips and snatches my bottle jokingly. She looks gently at me, and her heart and tone softens. "You lucky you ain't got no ugly baby." She starts feeding me, and the quiet calms Kristina. She watches Jasmine and wonders if she looks as comfortable holding and feeding me.

Jasmine looks back at her and says, "Don't you get no ideas. I am done after this. This is all the aunty duties I am doing for today." Kristina laughs and says, "Thank you. I really do appreciate it." The women exit the room and come into the living room. Kristina takes me to have me burp, and Jasmine says, "Babies are a lot of work, girl. But they sure are cute!"

"Yeah, they are cute until you don't sleep for three days."

"Where is your husband? Aren't you getting help from family?"

"What family, his mom? He had to take on extra loads because his dad is going through problems with scheduling."

"Sounds like his daddy needs to hire more people."

"Yes, when I mention it, I am just told that his father is doing the best he can."

"I know that gets old."

"And it does. But what can I do? He is the only one working, and that means I have to be here."

"At home with a baby, by yourself."

"Well, my mother-in-law comes, but it seems like she is trying to force her ideas on me. She wants me to do things her way. I just don't want to do that."

"I can understand that. Too many lioness make a den complicated. So, what do you want?"

"I honestly would love to go out and feel free for a few hours. Being cooped up in this house all day with the baby is starting to feel, "suffocating. I pray I don't sound selfish."

"You do a little bit, but that's a good thing. You have to care about yourself, or you can never be there for her. I ain't mad at you; I think it is healthy."

"So, you think I should go out?"

"How you going to do that? You are a momma and a wife now. You are right where you chose to be. I mean, some women want this life, although I am not sure why."

"Yeah."

Jasmine, reading the room, says, "But if you want to go out, I can hang with you."

"Okay, yeah, I was thinking we could go bowling or to the movies or something."

"Girl, we are not on a date. I was thinking more like out to dinner, to the club, or to go chill."

"So, what would I do with the baby? I can't bring her to the club, Jasmine."

"Yes, you cannot. So maybe you should wait until your husband comes home, and we do a girl's trip or something."

"Girl, I would be waiting for forever for that to happen. But I can get my mother-in-law to watch her for me."

"Okay, let me go get my clothes because I ain't going in this. I need to go home and change." Looking Kristina over, she says, "You, you need to change too. You ain't going nowhere with me looking like that. You look tired." Kristina throws a pillow at her and starts laughing with her.

Jasmine leaves, and Kristina is back alone with this baby, me. She calls my grandma and says, "Hey, Mom, how are you doing?"

"I am doing fine. How's my grandbaby?"

"She is good. Can I ask you a favor?"

"Sure, what do you need?"

"My mom needs me to come over to help her with a few things, and I wanted to know if you could watch Kimberly for me?"

"How long are you going to be?"

"She asked me to drive her around and go back and forth to her storage. So it might be either late this evening, or I can come first thing in the morning."

"So you want me to keep her overnight?"

"Yes, just this once. I was thinking when I got home, I could take a good bath and get some sleep. I've been struggling to stay awake today, and I figured I could use the time to sleep a bit."

"Oh, yes, I know it has been hard with your husband on the road too. So yeah, I will keep her tonight, and you can come in the morning. My husband won't be home until about two in the afternoon, so just be sure to get her before then. We have a dinner date later."

"Do you mind coming to get her for me? I was planning to clean up a bit before I left here."

"No, I'm out already, so I can swing by you now and get her. Just have her car seat ready; G-Ma has plans. I have some ladies that want to see her, and I can just bring her with me."

"Thanks, Mom." 'Freedom, Freedom' seemed to keep singing in Kristina's ear. She was excited for the first time in weeks. She didn't know why she was so happy; she didn't even like clubbing.

Her birthday was a dud because she was pregnant and home. Her husband took her out to dinner, but it was nothing like she imagined for turning twenty-one. She wasn't expecting a wild night, but she did want to drink at least.

Her mother-in-law seemed to have darted to her house. She rang the bell, and everything she needed was already packed and at the door. Kristina was cleaning and getting things ready because she knew her husband was likely coming home at the same time as his father. She and Gerald don't talk as much on the phone either because she ignores the call or because he avoids it so as not to hear her speak about how selfish he is.

The two of them had two separate viewpoints on each other's behaviors, and the phone calls that should have been about the love they had for their daughter turned into them nitpicking the small things that were growing into giants. As soon as I was gone, Kristina headed to her closet to see what she would wear. She thought of something light, fun, and not revealing.

She got her shirt on but didn't have time to put on the pants before Jasmine showed up dressed to the nine on cue. She smelled like candy and wore this bright but muted pink skirt, heels, and a jean jacket. She also wore a long blond curly hair weave.

Looking at her, she made Kristina change her mind on what to wear instantly. Kristina thought, dang, I am becoming a stay-at-home wife who only raises children for real, for real. She was losing touch with fashion and the outside world and didn't like it. She knew she needed to go out tonight.

The ladies finished playing dress up so they can go out. This time, Kristina was sure to bring her own purse, keep her phone, and drive her car.

They headed to several clubs but ended up going to the same one that they started with last time. Kristina really didn't want to go back to that same club because of the experience, but the music was wack at the others, and nobody showed up. Jasmine did not like partying alone, so she bar-hopped until she came back here.

When they arrived this time, Kristina got the same band as Jasmine, and the guard commented, "I remember you. Welcome back, and happy birthday." She responded, "Thank you." Her birthday was some time ago now, but she wanted to live the day she should have had on her birthday. It was going to be a good night, and she was going to enjoy it.

The music was blasting, and the lights were circling to the beat. The music did make you want to bop even if you didn't know who was rap-singing to the track. They headed to the bar, and Jasmine ordered for the both of them. She got the drinks and gave my mom hers. Kristina took a sip and realized it had alcohol. "Girl, I can't drink this; I gotta drive home."

"It's one drink. You will be fine."

"But I don't drink."

"You will today. It's your birthday! Enjoy yourself, and stop overthinking and just have fun." Kristina takes the drink back to her lips and sips some more. She feels a tap on her shoulders and swings around to see a familiar, handsome face. "Hey, I haven't seen you in a minute. How you been?" Jasmine whispers in her ear, "Please don't tell him you've been home raising children." She excuses herself and heads to the bathroom.

"No, I've just been busy working. How about you?"

"I've been chilling. Working, doing the same." They both drink their drinks and continue in small conversation. Jasmine sees them and intentionally spots a friend over by the door. "So you want me to get you another one? You look done."

"No, I was only drinking one. I drove."

"You got time, it's early. Another one, you should still be able to drive."

"I don't know, but thanks."

"It's cool; I will get another one too." He walks over to the bartender and orders two more drinks. They both cheer and take a sip when they bring their glasses down. Casually, they engage in some more light conversation. "So, what you out here doing tonight?"

"I am out here celebrating my birthday."

"Word?"

"Yeah, I turned twenty-one a few weeks back, and I wanted to make up for it."

"You didn't do anything on your birthday?"

"Naw, I was working and with family, but nothing special."

"Well, let me make sure this day is special. Hurry up and drink that. I got something you should try." He tips the drink toward her mouth, and she downs the drink. He goes back to the bartender and orders something blue. She asked, "What is it?"

He replies, "Just try it and let me know if you like it." She looks at him, and he says, "I will drink it to show you it is cool." He drinks from the cup and gives it back. She starts sipping it and says, "Oh, this is real good."

"I told you. So you ready to go dance?"

"Dance?"

"Yeah, dance." He takes her gently by the hand and they move toward a crowded place on the dance floor. The music seemed to get louder, and she couldn't hear Javier if he spoke a word. But she felt his hand drop down to her fingertips as he swung her towards him on the floor.

He pulled her closer and whispered in her ear, "You're going to have to help me. I can't dance." She laughed, and he took her arm and put it around his neck. As she held him around the neck, with the rhythm of the music, she swerved her hips, and his hands drifted to rest on her hips. The two of them stood eye to eye, dancing until Kristina slipped.

At that moment, Javier grabbed her in just enough time to reach for her shirt. As she was going down, his hand was trying to yank her back up, but the end result was her falling and hitting the floor. The sticky floor, which was also wet and she knew was filled with unforeseen germs, irked every fiber in her being. She tried to get up but couldn't gather her feet underneath her. She did a slow blink, but it didn't keep the room from spinning.

Javier reached down to pick her up from the floor, but as he was pulling her up, he realized she was not steady. He ushered her off the floor and asked, "Hey, are you good?"

"I think so. I just slipped."

"Yeah, I saw it. But I wasn't sure how you did that. I didn't see anything on the floor."

"Yeah, it was because the floor was wet, I think."

"Yeah, but did you see your shirt?"

"Naw, is something on my shirt?"

"Baby girl, your shirt ripped when I tried to keep you from falling." Kristina looks down and realizes her shirt is ripped. Embarrassed, she tries to cover her exposed areas. He takes off his outer layer shirt and gives it to her. Here, you can put this on."

She takes the shirt but struggles to put it on. She can't seem to find the holes for the arms. Javier helps usher her arms into the arm holes and asks her, "Hey, do you know where your friend is?"

"No, I haven't seen her since, uh, since…earlier."

"Yeah, I haven't seen her either. Do you want to call her and see where she's at?" Kristina reaches for her purse, but the chain-link purse is open. Her stuff hit the floor, and Javier reaches down to help her pick up things that just fell. She keeps looking into the purse and bringing it closer to her face. "Hey, did you see my, my, uhm, my keys?"

"Your keys?"

"Yeah, I had my keys in my purse."

"No, I checked the floor when you fell, just now was just paper. So they must have fallen out and slid." He hands her the paper.

"Can you, um, can you help me find my keys?"

"Yeah, of course." He turns around and starts

looking at the floor. He thought that Kristina was following behind him, but she wasn't. She had been walking, but another guy grabbed her by the hand and was trying to talk to her. She couldn't make out what he was saying, and he wanted to bring her closer to speak in her ear, but Javier came and pulled her away.

"Hey, you good?"

"Yeah, I'm good. Did you find, find my keys?"

"Oh, yeah, naw, I didn't see them. But were you ready to go home?"

"I mean, I need to find Jasmine. You think she is still even here? Or she left you again?"

"I don't know. Well, I can get you home."

"But I drove."

"I don't think you should be driving."

"But I can get a ride back. You want to call it for me?"

"Do you know your address?"

"Yeah, well, if you know your address, I can just drop you off at home. I don't think it is safe for you to be tipsy and be getting into a car with a stranger."

"You are a stranger."

"Really, you still think we are strangers?" he says jokingly.

Kristina laughs and responds, "Yeah, you

cool. You can take me home. I feel wet."

"You sure you didn't pee on yourself and that's not water?" She jokingly laughed, but she honestly wasn't sure. She was a bit out of sorts.

Kristina slips again, but this time, he catches her as they walk toward the exit. As he walks supporting her body, he sees Jasmine at the bar but ducks past her. They get outside, and the cool breeze seems to ignite a new personality in Kristina. She starts to dance when there is no music, and her feet seems to have instantly gotten weights tied about her ankles.

"Hey, where did you say you lived again?" Kristina rattled off her address before tripping on a crack in the sidewalk. Her knees hit the ground because Javier was looking around for his car, and his eyes were not set on her. Turning around, he helped to pull her back up. Pressing the button on his key fob, his car finally beeps to alert its location. He helped her to the car and stuck her down in the seat.

He went to the driver's seat and reached past her chest to buckle her seatbelt and then his own. He turned the ignition, and the two traveled to her house. He arrived at her house and helped her out of the vehicle. She had fallen asleep on the journey home, and she was quickly awakened when the breeze blew into her face.

It was as if her body got a second wind. She walked with her chest forward, unaware that her shoes had slipped off in the car, so she was barefoot. He made sure she arrived at her unit, and he used the spare key under the flower pot to open the door. She walked inside and fell onto the couch. He locked the door behind him.

Kristina woke up late that morning. My mom looked at the clock on her phone, which read 1:45pm. She rubbed her eyes and thought, there was something I was supposed to do. She heard and remembered it was something but couldn't place her finger on whatever it was. She sat up and knew her brain needed coffee to organize her thoughts.

She made a quick stop to the bathroom and then entered the kitchen. Then she saw someone and said, "Hey, I didn't know you would be home this early. How was the drive-in?" She went to grab a coffee cup and closed the door. When she looked up, the face was foreign. She dropped the cup, and he caught it and said, "Good Morning, sleepy. I made you breakfast. I pray you didn't mind."

"What are you doing in my house? How did you get in here?" She goes to a drawer and starts rummaging things around.

"Woe, don't get a knife. I brought you home last night. You lost your keys. Remember, you couldn't find stuff that fell out of your purse? Don't you remember?" He says, moving his arms as a desperate means to calm her nerves and keep her from moving around any more items in the drawer.

"What?"

"We hung out last night at the club. I gave you a ride home so you wouldn't be strained. Your car is still at the club. We couldn't find your keys last night."

"My car is left where?"

"At the club."

"Look, I need you to take me to my car right now."

"Yeah, sure. Of course." He picks up the plate, and she says, "There is no time for that, but thanks." The two of them head out the door so she could find her car. They arrive at the nightclub together, and she tries the door, but it is locked. She walks around back, but no answer. She tries to call Jasmine in hopes that she will have an update on where her keys are. But she, too, didn't pick up.

"Hey, if you need me to hang around to ensure you're good, let me know."

"No, just give me a minute to think. I don't understand how I have my house key but don't have my car key. It doesn't make sense."

"We used your spare key, which I found under the pot."

"Okay, well, thanks for helping me. I am going to call Pop a Lock or something until I can get the club to give me my stuff back. Wait, you said my ID was left here, too?"

"Yes, I think all your stuff fell out when you were dancing, and you fell."

"I fell?"

"Yea, nothing too crazy. You slipped, and I think all your stuff fell out of the little purse."

"Okay, thanks, what time is it?"

"2:45."

"Aww, shoot!"

"Something wrong?"

"Yes, I have to go pick up my daughter and meet my husband."

"Right, family stuff."

"Oh, I didn't ask, we are good, right? I mean, nothing happened between the two of us last night, right?"

"Do you remember anything happening?"

"Honestly, no, but I need you to say it."

"No, I just got you home, and you passed out on the couch. After that, I went to sleep, woke up at about 2:15, and cooked breakfast."

"Good, well, I got to go. I cannot be seen here with you. I mean no disrespect. I just don't want people getting the wrong idea."

"Of course, happy to help."

She steps off and calls her mother-in-law. The phone rings, and she picks up. "Hey, where are you? I thought you would be here by 2?"

"I got tied up and went to sleep late. We had a few more things to get done today. I apologize, but I am running behind."

"No problem. Gerald took the baby with him when he got here. He should be heading to the house now."

"Okay, of course, thanks. I will give him a call to let him know where I am." She phones her husband. He picks up and says, "Hey, where are you? Still helping out mom?"

"Yeah, she asked me to run some errands with her yesterday, and I needed to get something done today for her. Sorry, I am running behind."

"It's all good, but I wished you would have told me."

"Yeah, sorry about that, honey. Just got a little distracted." Javier starts to walk up to her, and he says, "Hey, you almost–" She shakes her head for him to be silent, and he stops talking. "Yeah, so I am going to drop this off and head home. Give me about an hour."

Her husband replies, "Okay, see you when you get home."

The two hang up, and Javier hands her her shoes. "How do you have my shoes?" She takes her shoes from him, puzzled.

"You must have taken them off last night in my car. Don't worry, I am gone, and you don't have to see me again."

"I think that's for the best." He walks back to his car and drives off. She stands outside and thinks to phone for help to unlock her car and get home. She is still uncertain how she will drive her car back but knows she cannot leave it here. She calls Jasmine again, praying she will reach her, and good thing she answers.

"Hello?"

"Hey, it's Kristina."

"Well, look who is calling after her night of shame?"

"What are you talking about?"

"You left me last night. I was searching the whole club for you."

"Yeah, I got a ride home. I was too drunk to drive."

"Yeah, you were so drunk you forgot to tell me you were leaving. I saw you, though."

"Saw me what?"

"I saw you with the guy with the braids. So did y'all have a good time last night?"

"Nothing happened. He just drove me home, and we both fell asleep."

"We are both grown women. If you don't want to tell me what happened, just say that."

"Why would I lie? We didn't have sex, Jasmine."

"Hmmh uhn. Okay, sure. So where are you now?"

"I am back at the club."

"Why are you there? Ain't nobody going to be there until this evening."

"I left my ID and my keys."

"Now, how did you do that?"

"I fell last night, and all of my stuff came out of my purse." Jasmine starts laughing.

"You really sounding like a sad story. You shouldn't get drunk in public if you are losing stuff and having strange men drive you home."

"I need you to do me a favor."

"What kind of favor?"

"My husband cannot find out what happened last night, obviously. If you struggle to believe what happened, he certainly won't believe me. So I need to tow my car to your house and for you to drive me home."

"You said you need to tow your car here?"

"Yes, I cannot drive it, and I cannot leave it here either."

"Hey, whatever you need to do, I am here. Just give me a minute to get up. I will text you my address."

Relieved, Kristina calls the tow truck and gets a ride to Jasmine's house. She gives her a ton of thank yous. Later, Kristina arrives home. Gerald is sitting on the couch with something balled up in his hands. He doesn't look towards her, but he speaks from the couch.

"Kristina, what's going on?"

Kristina kicks her shoes off at the door and moves to go toward the couch. "Sorry, babe. My car wouldn't start at Jasmine's house. So I had her drive me over here. I was going to call you, but she said I could leave it there and come back for it. I think it is something simple anyway."

He doesn't want her to get close to him or near his proximity. She senses the hesitation and attempts to head to my bedroom, but Gerald stops her when he says, "Hold up a sec, she's good. I put her to sleep hours ago. Hey, did you say her name was Jasmine?"

"Yeah, Jasmine."

"Well, Jasmine, were you here last night?"

Like a deer in headlights, Jasmine's eyebrows went up, and she said, "Yes, I was here."

"Okay, so can you explain to me why you left your shirt on my kitchen table?" He opens the balled-up item, revealing a man-size undershirt.

"Uh"

"Look, you don't have to lie for her. No woman makes another woman breakfast and takes off their shirt. This man's shirt was on my kitchen table. You forgot about our daughter, and you look like hell. You want to tell me where the car is for real?"

"I told you, it is at Jasmine's house."

"Yes, it is at Jasmine's house now. But that is not where it was last night or this morning, and even up to about two hours ago. Kristina, wow. If you didn't want to be with me, why not tell me?"

Jasmine says, "Maybe I should go."

"No, you should stay," replies Gerald.

"What are you talking about?" says Kristina.

"I GPS your location last night when you dropped off our daughter, and I didn't know where you were. I called your phone, but you didn't answer. So I traced your phone and saw that you were at a club. I didn't trip because–I know you hung out with Jasmine before."

"So you spying on me?"

"I wouldn't have to if you was real. I know you and I haven't been working for weeks, but that doesn't mean you step out on me like this."

"First of all, I didn't cheat on you if that is what you think."

"Really?"

"Yes, I did get drunk last night. I came home late, but I was here."

"So you can explain why I found this in the bathroom trash can?" He pulls out an open condom wraper. "The rest was next to the bed. You nasty. And what is so messed up about this? You were so drunk you don't even know what you did last night. The neighbors say you thrown over a man's shoulder wearing no shoes. Y'all two were loud all night. I got the call, by the way, for the noise complaint this morning. And you and your little boyfriend can pay that bill."

"But right now, you are getting the hell out of here." He points to the two suitcases near the door. She hadn't noticed the suitcases before he mentioned them. She replies, "You can't do that, and, and– finding that doesn't prove anything. How do you know it wasn't someone else?"

"Come on, Kristina, can you just stop embarrassing yourself and making this worse?"

"I don't remember none of this."

"You know what is sad? I believe you. But the video I got was your nail in the coffin with me."

"What video?"

Gerald pushes buttons on his phone, and Kristina hears a beep. She looks at it, and it is a screen recording from their alarm system. The image shows her getting up from the couch and walking to the bedroom with the guy with the braids. She grabs his butt, and the two head into the bedroom, and the door is closed behind him.

"Babe, I don't remember none of this, and if anything happened, it was because I thought he was you."

"We haven't had sex in months. I don't know how long this fantasy of yours has been going on, but I don't care. You can get your stuff and get he hell out."

"This is my house too."

Raising his voice, his shoulders tense when he speaks, "Not anymore. Now get your stuff and get out!" Kristina jumps, and Jasmine grabs her by the arm. Jasmine helps her grab the two suitcases and moves her closer to the door.

"Hey, we need to go." She pulls Kristina by the arm as Gerlad starts to lose his composure. The two hurry down the steps, and Jasmine says, "Look, I am not a psych, but if a man starts crying, it is time to go."

Gerald sat there trying to compose himself. He wasn't sure of why he was crying. Even though he knew the marriage could have been over months ago, he didn't want to get a divorce or give up on his family. Seeing his little girl, he didn't want to break up the home he wanted to create, but after this, he couldn't see the family being put back together again. It was over, and now he was mourning the death of what could have been.

Kristina was quiet the entire car ride. She wasn't sure of what was happening and where things were for her. A part of her was relieved. She wasn't happy and hadn't been for a while. But this wasn't the way she wanted to obtain her freedom. She wanted to find that braided liar and give him a piece of her mind.

Although her life was flashing before her eyes, what she didn't immediately think about was me, her daughter, and how her selfishness blew up my world. This was the rain kicking up a lot, and this rain would lead to a downpour of events in my life. Things only got worse for the both of us. Her life was moving fast, and she started to cry. Jasmine asked, "Aww, it's okay. I am sure he just needs to calm down."

"But he is right. I haven't been happy for months. I didn't know how to tell him. I don't want this. I don't want to be a wife stuck at home with a baby. I want to be in school and make something for myself."

"I told you, ain't nothing wrong with being happy and living your life. Maybe this is the best thing for you. You are young, and you have your whole life to live. This could be a blessing in disguise."

"It is messed up. I am so embarrassed and–. I want to beat Javier in the face. Why would he lie?"

"All men lie."

"How could I be so stupid?"

"Maybe this needed to happen so you can have a clean break. It doesn't count if you don't remember it, anyway."

"Yes, it does. I might be getting a divorce because of it."

"I can't say anything there. I ain't married. But if you ain't happy, stop sweating it. Get your baby and just move on."

Then it hit her: how would she care for the baby herself? What would even Gerald do? He was never home, so that meant she would have to take care of me herself. Would her ex-mother-in-law help her now? She probably never cared for my mother for all the right reasons. How did she make her life go from bad to worse? She thought about it more and more. How was she going to take care of me by herself?

It was hell for Kristina for the next few weeks. The divorce proceedings were brutal, and she felt it was very unfair. She had a progressive judge who believed in fair treatment of both parents, so they got joint custody. Although she had primary custody, because he drove over the road most overnights. He, of course, was ordered to pay child support, but the double whammy was that she was ordered to pay alimony.

Although Gerald didn't ask for it, his lawyer pushed for it because she was unfaithful, and for everything he paid for the wedding, she argued he should get half of it back. The alimony was set at half the wedding cost, and she kept the apartment. The judge did give him up to ninety days to find a new place because of his crazy work schedule. Kristina lived with Jasmine while she rebuilt her life. It was a quick divorce because they weren't fighting for stuff, and everything was straightforward.

It broke Gerald's heart to come to an empty home when his daughter wasn't there. Many nights, Kristina wanted to call him because, somehow, being alone without him didn't feel right either. She missed the help of her ex-mother-in-law but knew she couldn't ask. She spent weeks trying to get into a rhythm.

Without a bed and a room, she was forced to care for me, living out of Jasmine's living room, which was getting old. Jasmine wanted her life back, and although she empathized with her friend, she couldn't live like this for much longer. Kristina had to snap out of the funk and get her stuff together—and quickly. She urged Kristina to have a conversation with Gerald so they could do what was best for Kimberly.

She needed to make more money now that she had to pay alimony. The alimony and child support payments were a wash, so she needed a higher-paying job. She was ready to go to medical coding school now because the old job wasn't cutting it. It was good timing when her income tax check came because it gave her the money to pay bills, and she moved back into the apartment.

Things were far from perfect, but they were getting to a good place. She enrolled Kimberly in a daycare not far from her house and began online classes. The program was eight weeks long, so she planned to have a job in the next ninety days, right around the time her money would get tight. She had a feeling one of her payments on something might lapse while she was looking for a new job, but she was willing to take the gamble.

It was her full-time job to dive into medical coding. She studied every moment she was not wiping snot buggers, cleaning the house, or caring for me. Her life of freedom felt like more stress, but she couldn't reverse time. She didn't love Gerald, so she didn't miss him personally, but she longed for the help, the break that didn't come often enough.

Every other weekend was the schedule for Gerald's pick-up. He hated the schedule. His schedule changed ever so often, so he couldn't make the pick-ups closer together until the business either hired more people or he got a new route. These months of adjustment were hard on both of them.

The person with the greatest impact from their break-up was me. I had my first birthday at two houses with close friends and family of the parent in attendance. It was too soon for the two of them to come together and plan anything. At this time, they didn't speak during drop-offs, and if they could have left me and my things outside the door and left, they would have.

I kept growing, and at this stage, I was getting into things and knocking a lot of stuff over. I was an adventurous baby who loved messing with anything that could make a mess, and my mother hated it. She wanted time to do more things for herself. She loved me but couldn't see how all the changes were taking a toll on her mental health. She needed a break and fast.

She begged her grandmother to take me for a night so she could go and have a little fun. She objected, but Kristina devised a plan. She went to her grandmother's house and sat down. She told me to go and play, and while I was playing in the other room, Kristina kicked up small talk with Grandma.

"So, Mom, how have you been?"

"You know, getting old is never easy. So, I take it a day at a time. I won't complain and give the devil glory. God is able to take care, you know?"

"Yes, He is. Are you taking your medications to deal with the pain?"

"You know I try to keep up with things. But it can be so much to remember. They still don't know why I have this pain in my legs and back. I have gotten injections and changed my medications so many times, but it is still there. I am just learning to live through it. If the Father's grace was sufficient for Paul, it has to be enough for me, too. So I am bearing with it."

"You want me to get you anything?"

"Yes, can you get me some water? I think I need to take something for my legs. It's like once you bring it up, that's when the pain strikes. Also, can you give me the remote? My nurse put it over there, and if I don't need to get up, I will just sit here a minute."

"Of course." Kristina grabs the remote and gives it to her. She heads into the kitchen and sits at the table for about five minutes. She gets up and looks in on her grandmother, who is nodding as she watches her episode. Her grandmother has always been a fan of sitting in front of the TV while it watches her fall asleep. She fills her glass and peeps in on me and sees me happily playing with some of Grandma's grandchildren's community toys.

She goes to the living room, and Grandma is out like a light. She places the glass on the table with a light thud as it hits the coffee table. Her grandmother moves slightly, but her eyes remain shut. Kristina backs away from the couch and practically runs out of the door. She eases the door shut, hops into the car, turns the keys in the ignition, and takes off. She wasn't sure where she wanted to go. She thought a bite of food would do the trick.

Her mom usually slept for a good hour or two before waking. The clock was ticking, and she wanted to be close in case she got an impromptu call. She went to the end of the street and turned into a local dinner. She took a deep inhale in the parking lot and exited the vehicle.

When she enters the door, the bells ring. A friendly waitress greets her and asks, "Are you dining in or taking it to go?"

"I will be dining in," she replied. The waitress smiles and tells her to follow her. On the way to her seat, she picks up a menu and greets her formally. The place was busy enough for the two servers, who seemed to be waiting on the entire restaurant alone. Dining out is nothing like it used to be before Covid. I guess good help is still hard to find, Kristina thought as she ordered her food.

She sat there looking around the restaurant, and for the first time, she realized that she was alone. Without the baby, who needed her to survive, she had nothing. She was always grateful for her grandmother, but she knew her age was creeping up.

The bell at the door rang as a gentleman with a familiar face walked in. It took her some time, but she recognized him. He was Javier from the club. At that moment, she debated whether she should approach him or hide behind something. Before she could decide, he approached her table.

"Hey, stranger. How have you been?"

"Homewrecker, I have been doing fine," retorts Kristina. Javier eases into the chair and replies, "Oooh, that sounds like bad news. But it wasn't me."

"It was you. You lied when I asked you if anything happened that night."

"Wait, what are you talking about? You mean we did something that night?"

"Yes, and it was caught in part on camera."

"I don't mean to offend you, but I don't

remember that night at all. I got you home and re-member crashing on the couch."

"Yeah, you left out how we went back to the bedroom after."

"Hey, is this some kind of –" Kristina inter-rupts, "No, it was me who led you to the bedroom." He replies, "You had me nervous. No means no. So, does it count if I don't remember?"

"That makes two of us because I don't re-member it either."

"Then, let's say it didn't happen. We were at least friends before, or were we not?" Kristina eye-balls him, and he leans in closer for encouragement. "Come on, you not my friend anymore because of a drunk night months ago? I tried to looking out for you but didn't see you. So I figured I would just see you around. I wasn't ghosting you."

"My life has been a nightmare lately. I just needed to clear my head. I didn't feel like dealing with whatever this was. I had intentions of confront-ing you, but the right time and place never came around." She sips her drink, and the waitress comes with her food. She asks, "Hey, can I get you any-thing?"

"Yeah, I will take an orange juice and the breakfast slam, please."

"You eat breakfast in the afternoon?"

"What do you think most men eat when they don't have a girl? Breakfast! At least it isn't a bowl of cereal." He looks to the waiter and answers her remaining questions about the order. Kristina starts to dig into her food, and Javier says, "Girl, you aren't going to pray over your food?"

84

"Don't be so old school. God knows I love Him."

The two kept on talking for another hour until she saw her grandma's number pop up on her phone. She purposefully ignored it. She knew her window was winding down for being free. But she was enjoying herself. It had been a moment since she honestly felt desired, and the feeling felt great.

"Hey, I gotta go." Javier looks concerned and jokingly says, "Am I running you off again?"

"No, I got to go pick up my daughter."

"Oh, okay, children are the future. I understand. So hey, what are you doing tomorrow?"

"Home and work is my life now."

"Don't you think you should have a life outside of work and home? I mean, you are a woman with needs–who has friends."

"Don't be slick."

"Naw, I'm just saying you are young and pretty. Any smart man would want to take you out. Seriously. I would love to take you out when you are free again."

"It could be a minute."

"I will wait. Good things are worth waiting for."

"Charming and cute. I can't say more–"

"You'll be able to soon enough."

"What makes you so sure there will be a next

time?"

"Because I think you like me. But to know you like me, I am going to put my number in your phone. If you like me, you will call me when you got some time. Anytime, day or night, works for me."

Kristina lets him take her unlocked phone out of her hand. He puts in his number and inserts a blue heart at the end of his name. "I put a heart on there so you know it's me in case you got a lot of brothers trying to holla at you. I know you ladies always say you ain't got nobody chasing, but I want to be clear. I like you–and not in no friendly way. I can see a future with us."

She smiles and says, "Alright, Blue. I will see you later. I gotta go." She stands up from the table, and he gently grabs her hand. He leans in and kisses her on the cheek. "Thanks for the first date, beautiful."

"Date?"

"We met at a restaurant, ate good food, talked, laughed, and I paid the check. Sounds like a date to me. Now, I just need to know if we will have another one?" Kristina giggles and walks away, smiling on the outside and inside.

Moments later, she arrives at her grandma's house. She sees Gerald's car out front and gets out in a hurry. Gerald is closing the backseat door, and Kimberly is already inside the car. Kristina asks, "Hey, what are you doing here?"

"No, the question should be, why weren't you here?"

"Because I went around the corner to get something to eat."

"Oh really? I have been sitting here for over an hour. I should have been driving out to work, but I got a call from your mother telling me she didn't know where you were. You still don't change, I see. You're lying."

"I was around the corner, and I don't have to explain my whereabouts to you!"

"No, you don't. But when you left our child with your mother, who didn't know where you went, that matters. She did not agree to watch our daughter, and she called me looking for you! Look, I don't know if you got a boyfriend or something, but I don't want your bad choices impacting our daughter. If you need to duck off somewhere and do whatever, just let me know. I don't mind taking care of my daughter."

"She is our daughter, Gerald. I went out for an hour or two, and you guys are fussing me out? What, I can't go anywhere because you two think I can't?"

"No, I don't care what you do, let's be clear. I do, however, care about who is watching my daughter–excuse me, our daughter. Your mother can't stay up, and you know she is in a lot of pain. What would make you think bringing Joy (me, my dad's nickname for me) here was fair to her or your mother? She has been here crying for who knows how long. Her pull up is full, and your mom didn't know she was even there. She didn't change or check on her. I don't know when she ate or nothing."

He goes on to say, "I don't know what kick you are on, Kristina, but this is not good."

"Look, I just wanted to get out and have a little Me time."

"Well, why don't you take the night or–hell, the weekend? I missed my shift. Go do whatever we interrupted you from doing. We will see you later." Gerald enters the car, closes the door, and watches Kristina walk up to the car in protest. He then drives off down the street, paying her no mind.

Kristina dreadfully entered the house and spotted her grandmother sitting in her chair with her head looking straight at the door. Kristina looked down at the floor, and before she could say a word, her grandmother said, "What the hell is wrong with you, Kristina? I had no idea you left the baby here with me. I don't know how long you have been gone, and I told you I was not able to watch your baby. I love you, but this was dangerous."

"Ma, I was around the corner at the dinner. I was only gone for about two hours."

"Yeah, but I didn't know you were gone for two hours. What if she would have turned on the stove or gotten into products in the bathroom? You can't just leave toddlers to deal with themselves. You should have told me you were leaving. Furthermore, you should have regarded my wishes and taken your baby with you when you left. After today, I don't trust you, Kristina. This was selfish of you."

"It really wasn't that big of a deal. I think you both are overreacting."

"Look, I don't know what is going on with you and how you think this is okay. But it is not. Now get out of my house."

"Really? You are going to throw me out, Ma?"

"I don't want to see your face right now. I am sitting here in pain. I can barely walk. How are you expecting me to watch your daughter when I told you I couldn't–because of what?"

"I just need some time to clear my head."

"Why not call her father? Or his mother?"

"They are busy, and he has been taking on more shifts. He barely has time for her."

"Well, he helps with paying his support. Put her in daycare."

"She is but only for a certain time. I can't afford full time. I have to watch how much money I spend while I'm in school."

"Ask her father for more."

"He is still helping with the rent. I can't ask him for more."

"Then figure it out. You can go get state assistance."

"I ain't poor. I don't want no government checks. I am going to do this."

"I think that is stupid; you need help but refuse it from people who can help you. Instead, you sneak around, leaving her anywhere–"

"Look, you don't have to worry about me no more, Grandma. I will call you to check on you, but I won't be back."

"I ain't saying you can't come back. I am saying I need a minute. You scared me today, and the way you are acting, this isn't you."

"Maybe it is the me I am becoming. People

grow up, Mom."

"Yeah, they do, but this wasn't that. And whatever this is, I want no parts of it. Gone on." Kristina turned her back toward her grandmother and high-stepped out the door. She thought of driving home but didn't want to be reminded of how lonely it would be. She called Jasmine, but she didn't pick up.

She stopped having friends years ago from high school, and she could think of no one else to phone as she drove the streets looking for love, acceptance, or just a friend.

When Kristina gets home, she goes inside. The house is quiet. She has longed for quietness, but this isn't the way she wanted it. It feels like she lost something, although she is not sure of what. She grabs some ice cream from the fridge and turns on the tv. It's early, and after three episodes of her favorite season, the sun going down seems to welcome her to sleep.

At that moment, she realizes she is no different from her grandmother. She is sitting alone, watching the tv as she falls asleep. As she reflects, a few tears drop from her face, and she picks up her phone to check the time. When she looks, she sees Javier's name with the blue heart.

She hesitates as she glares at her phone through tears. She pushes the call button and his phone rings. When she thinks about hanging up, she hears, "Hello?"

"Uh, hey."

"Yea, what up?" replied Javier.

"It's Kristina."

"Hey, girl. I thought it would have been a minute till I heard from you."

"I guess you made an impression."

"Okay, I like that. So what are you up to?"

"Nothing, just sitting on the couch watching tv."

"Sounds like a Netflix and chill kind of night."

"Yeah, but it is a bit too chill."

"You got time to hang out tonight?"

"If you are up for date two?"

"Of course. When do you want to link?"

"Well, I am free now."

"I can come by you if you're cool with that?"

"Yeah, I will send you the address. I may need to change."

"Yeah, put on something nice. We are going to have a good time tonight. You can trust me."

She smiles and replies, "I better." They chat a bit more as she searches her closet for something to wear. She hung up, and it was like she zeroed in on what to wear at that moment. It was a sequenced black dress with silver accents. She wore the perfect heels to match. She oiled up her legs, lotioned her arms and elbows, and added moisture to her face. She looked like new money but needed to do her hair and face.

She entered the bathroom and applied a gel-like pencil liner that seemed to glide on perfectly. She normally has a slight wave, but today, she nailed it. She added soft pink and gray eyeshadow and elevated the colors on the lid. She put a brown highlighter on her cheeks and a gold bronzer down her nose and under her eyes. Lastly, she added mascara, and the look was finished!

Now to the hair. Kristina loved different quick weaves, especially with the time she had to get dressed. She decided to change up the color and wear a wig that would pop the color of her skin. She wore a red twenty-two-inch special she picked up on sale that she never wore. In fact, most things in her closet she had when she was married, she never wore. It felt good to wear some of it tonight.

She was dressed and thought of sitting on the couch and waiting for her date. Sitting around and waiting for someone in her own house felt weird, but as she reached the living room, there was a knock at the door. She checked the door and opened it to see Javier there with flowers.

"Wow, thank you! How did you have enough time to get flowers.?"

"I can't tell you all of my secrets. But dang girl, I wasn't talking about this fly. I was expecting a cute, chill look."

"Well, it was some things I had lying around."

"Okay, let's go see what the night brings then. You hungry?"

"Yeah, I think so. I haven't eaten since earlier today."

"Well, I got a nice spot for us."

The two of them head out the door. Javier

puts his hand around Kristina's small waist as they walk toward the car. She didn't remember his car as much from before. She didn't notice he drove a dark blue Mercedes. She is impressed, but she doesn't say a word. Her smile is sufficient for Javier, so he doesn't push for compliments.

He opens the door for her, and she takes her seat while her dress hikes up to show her upper thigh. Javier tingles at the sight and grins. He walks over to his side of the car, sits inside, turns the ignition, and the two of them take off. Something about the air in this car feels light. It feels euphoric and rich, and it is something Kristina longed for.

Although the day quickly shifted towards night, she enjoyed looking out the window to see the sun dropping. Javier opened the roof and pulled the windows down slightly. The breeze was perfect, blowing across her face. As she continues to look out the window, the music turns up a bit more as they cruise, and she feels his hand gently rest upon her knee. In the moment, it didn't bother her. She just wanted to soak in the moment.

They took a twenty-minute drive and pulled up to a lively restaurant featuring a live band. The atmosphere was mood-setting, lowly light, with people smiling and enjoying each other's company. Her ex had never taken her to this restaurant. He thought it was dumb to waste money on places that cooked the same food for three times the price as others.

Kristina quickly pushed the comparison out of her mind and allowed Javier to take her by the hand to the hostess stand. He put their names on the list. While they waited, they went to the bar for a drink. "Hey, what are we drinking tonight?"

"Good one. I don't know if I should drink

anything with you." She said jokingly.

"Come on, I got you. We are here to relax. Do you have somewhere to be tomorrow?"

"No."

"So let's live, enjoy, and be grown. Trust the vibe."

"Alright, well, pick something for me."

He looked over the menu and settled on two colorful drinks from the drink special. The glasses were quickly served, and the two giggled for thirty minutes while they waited for their table, the time flew by. The hostess called for them and escorted them to their table. They were quickly greeted by their server, who asked for their drink orders. He ordered them a bottle of mixed-blend red wine.

Kristina was surprised she liked it. She had never had wine before, but she liked the first one. As she sipped her wine, he looked at her and asked, "So, how are you doing?"

"What do you mean?"

"You look great, but I figured something might have happened to make you call me. So I had to ask, you good?"

"I just had a run-in with my daughter's father. He thought all the wrong things. I hate when people are so selfish and only see things from their perspective. I wasn't happy in our marriage for a long time, but I stayed. I tried. We were just too different, and he worked too much. We barely saw each other, so naturally, we drifted."

"Yeah, I can see that. So, did you ever tell

him you weren't happy?"

"Not openly, no. But we stopped having sex months before we divorced. After the baby came, I just didn't feel like it anymore."

"Dang, he stayed with you and never stepped out?"

"I don't know. I wasn't on the road with him. But I don't think he did. Gerald is the loyal type."

"So if you got a good man, why do you feel you couldn't work things out?"

"Do you think I should be with Gerald right now?"

"Come on, easy. I am just saying women out here looking for a good dude to marry them."

"Well, he can go and find a perfect woman for him now that he is free from the wicked and selfish woman that I am."

"No, that's not what I meant. What I want to say, I think you are a beautiful woman. You are definitely a catch, and he was right to swoop you up and marry you. I don't knock him. Maybe you were too much for him, and you got bored with what he didn't have. Some women just need more than a man can give."

"Okay, I like that. I do feel like even during our honeymoon, we had problems and red flags. I just didn't want to bail on him. He didn't have the money to give me what I wanted and dreamed of. I wanted this grand wedding, but it just didn't happen. He seemed to get mad at me because what we wanted wasn't what he wanted to pay."

She went on to say, "I mean, weddings are supposed to last forever. We get married one time. Was it really too much to spend about twenty thousand on a wedding?"

"You spent twenty thousand dollars on your wedding?"

"Almost, more like about seventeen."

"I heard weddings can be about twenty to thirty thousand for most couples. So you saved some money."

"That's what I thought." The food arrived at the table, and the two cheered as Javier poured their second round from the bottle. They smiled and enjoyed each other's company. Javier seemed to know the perfect time to grab Kristina's free hand as they discussed their lives. Something about him made her comfortable.

They enjoyed a glass of wine while they had dessert. The two of them were stuffed, and he asked if she wanted to go dancing. She replied, "I am so full I don't feel like doing that."

He replied, "Do you want to go for a walk? I know this nice place–"

She interrupts him and says, " With these shoes, I think you should take me home. I know I am not supposed to say this, but my feet are killing me. They are new, and these straps feel like they are digging into my skin."

"Okay, well, let's make an emergency stop at your house and see what you want to do after that." They agreed he grabbed the check, and the two headed to her house. As a gag, he picked her up, threw her over his shoulder, and brought her to her door. She entered the house and quickly plopped down on the couch to remove her shoes.

He picks up her foot and starts to massage it. He seems to have magic hands as he works the stress from the soles of her feet, toes, and ankles. It was a nice surprise to feel his hands move up to her calves. She is vibing and enjoying the moment. She knows the rules her grandmother taught her, but tonight, she wants to be in the moment and not overthink it. She should make him wait, but why if it feels right?

He moved up past her knee and firmly gripped her thigh. The gentle, firm pressure made her melt like butter in his warm hands. Something about the grip made her body lean into the caress. Her body was arrested as he moved to her other thigh, balancing the motion. Her eyes closed, and her body relaxed even more.

He leans her body back onto the couch and rotates her around. Laying on her stomach, his hands start at her shoulder and firmly press her neck. The confident grip makes her submit to his direction. She moans in response, and he rubs his hands down her back, moving down every curb. Her body needed this release of stress.

Each caress removed several insecure moments from her mind, and she replaced the memories of old with new ones, filled with lighthearted and easy fun. Life had been hard, filled with overthinking and yearning for more. At this moment, she wanted nothing more except more time. The night was young, and she had nothing to do the next day.

As he finished caressing her lower back, he grabbed her backside, clearly enjoying the hold. It was not a professional touch but filled with longing. She turned under his guidance, and he began with her temple. He massaged her face, moving every concern, and an unexpected tear dropped that he noticed. He kissed away her tears without saying a word. He might not have known it, but it was the perfect response.

She reached for him, and he placed his face in her hands. She kissed him gently, and the kisses grew firmer and more passionate. The spark quickly turned into a roaring blaze between them, and they exchanged kisses and touches on the couch in the low light; they spoke no words.

Moans did the talking, and the early sunrise welcomed their bodies to rest. For several hours, they both muted the world and troubles around them. It was just the two of them, and they enjoyed every moment, hour, second they shared.

Last night was perfect, and Kristina wanted the cloud she was on to last. She had no reason to rush him off, so the two enjoyed going to breakfast that late afternoon when they awoke. The two of them kidded around and took the walk he intended for them to have the night prior at the park. He enjoyed watching the children play as they sat on the bench.

Kristina talked about the struggles of being a mom and how he wasn't missing out on not being a father yet. He told her that someday, he would love to have lots of girls. He felt that he was meant to be a girl dad. She laughed and felt genuinely happy. She had work tomorrow and was uncertain about how the week would play out.

She was likely to get a call from Gerald to either come and get Kimberly or that he was dropping her off. Surprisingly, she didn't hear from him until Thursday. She invited her new lover over every night and thought to have him out early mornings, but she had no reason to rush. That Thursday, Gerald said he would bring her by later that week because she was spending time with his mother.

My mom couldn't have been more pleased. She and Javier spent each night together for that extended period of time, and their bond proliferated. It was surprising how much time the two spent and how quickly they fell into each other's world. The movies they picked would often watch them into the early morning.

Javier getting to work from her house in the mornings was a test with the traffic and travel time. Yes, Kristina didn't know much about him, but for the moment, she wanted to ride the wave and enjoy what they were experiencing. She felt light as a feather. Gerald recognized her mood when he dropped off their daughter that Tuesday.

Although Kristina was very comfortable with Javier, she didn't think introducing him to her daughter was a good idea. So that weekend, she felt lonely again, even missing his company. It was strange for her to miss him so much when things between them were still new.

His sentiment was similar. Quickly, she slid into his heart, and he didn't move to pump the brakes.

The months ahead were filled with early morning departures from Javier before Kimberly could wake up. Kristina was enjoying the freedom of having a life. She also knew her daughter was growing up, and Gerlad might have questions soon. It was strange how fast the weeks turned into months. Kimberly was growing quickly and changing. Kristina's life was also about to take a drastic turn.

I learned to walk weeks after my first birthday. If things were busy before, now that I was trying to nail talking and putting together sentences, my mom struggled all the more to keep me in one place. She was already bumping heads with me, and my explorative nature and the sass I had could only be described as being inherited from her.

It was a late night when a knock was at the door. It was a slightly early evening compared to normal. Kimberly was still up and getting out of her bath. Kristina wrapped the toddler up in a towel and went to answer the door. Unsurprisingly, it was Javier, but she wasn't sure if she should introduce them without proper time to think.

There was another knock at the door, and she opened it. "Hey, Javier, can you give me a second? I just got my daughter out of the tub." She looks at Kimberly and says, "Kimmie, this is Javier,

Mommy's friend." Javier reaches out his hand, and Kimberly stares at him.

Kristina takes me by the hand and extends it toward Javier. He takes my hand and kisses it on the back of my hand. I yanked it back. Kristina replies, "Sorry, she started daycare but she is still only used to family. If you give me a moment, I will put her to bed."

"It's cool. I don't mind helping. I told you I want to be a girl-dad. Anything I can do to help?"

"No, not really. I am just going to put her clothes on."

"Okay, I will just hang around and watch. If you need an extra pair of hands, let me know."

"Well, thank you." They all walk into Kimberly's room, and Javier sits in the rocking chair. He looks on from the back of the room as Kristina cares for her daughter. She gets me dressed quickly and puts me in the bed. My mother lifted the sheet to cover my body and said, "Night, night, Kimmie."

Javier pops up from the chair, walks over to the bed, and says, "Good night, Kimmie. He taps her on her hand lying on the bed to show his sincerity." She closes her eyes and doesn't say a word in return. The two of them leave my room and close the door.

"Sorry, she is not as sociable as I expect sometimes."

"No, kids have their own mind. Every one of them is different. No problem. So, how are you doing today?"

"Good. I think I am just about ready to take my test. I have been studying for about a month now. I cannot put it off any longer if I want to get a good-paying job."

"Yeah, well, what do you think about me helping out more?"

"What are you talking about?"

"I mean, I don't want you to feel rushed to take your test because of money. Correct me if I am wrong, but you have to pay for the test?"

"Yeah, I have to pay for four of them. But when I do, money can be tight for a bit."

"I can give you some money."

"I don't know how I feel about that."

"I am here all the time. I feel bad that I spend so much time here and I am not paying rent. It's cool."

"You sure?"

"Yeah, if you want me to move in so you feel better about taking my money, just say the word. But I am here for you and little Kimmie. She is so gorgeous. And her eyes are breathtaking."

"Well, thank you. She is cute. I am grateful she looks a lot like me."

"She does. She is like your twin but about twenty-five years younger."

"Hey, that sounded like a diss."

"No, I just can see a future for her. I am looking at her."

Kristina smiles, and she starts undoing his shirt. She starts admiring his tattoos. "You know, I have been meaning to ask you. Do some of your tattoos mean anything?"

"Some do, some I just like the design."

"What does this tattoo mean?"

"Oh, the Medusa tattoo?"

"Yeah, isn't that the lady who kills people with her eyes?"

"Yeah, that's her. She was one of my favorite characters."

"But why do you have the snakes like this?"

"Yeah, I think the snakes symbolize my victories."

"But the snake bodies are missing the head."

"Yeah, because I killed them. You can look into her eyes if she didn't have the snake heads. Her eyes are so beautiful, so why miss it."

"If you say so," replies Kristina as Javier moves his arm to kiss her. The two of them have their own party for two well into the evening. The next day, they all go to the park together to enjoy the sun.

The walk to the park was brief. Javier seemed to be a hit with the mothers at the park. He was willing to help the girls up to the top of the slide for those who permitted him to help. He played around the playground set with Kimmie as she went up the ladder and down the slide.

They stayed at the park for about thirty minutes before going to a local restaurant for lunch. They all enjoyed their meals and desserts. Then, they walked down the street and headed back home.

When they got home, Javier suggested they watch a movie. So the three of them piled up on the couch, with Kimmie sitting on Javier's lap and Kristina sitting to his right. The three watched a children's movie together and laughed until their eyes got heavy. Kimmie had fallen asleep first. Javier, thinking he wanted some alone time with Kristina, got up to put her in bed.

He returned to the living room after kissing her on the forehead. He eased back into his position on the couch after slightly lifting Kristina's head. She shuffled to get more comfortable, and he sat there watching her sleep so beautifully. The only thing to make the moment better would be to see her beautiful eyes gazing up at him.

He could sit for hours looking into her eyes. Something about them made him feel loved and welcomed. He wanted to always to be in her arms and around her. To make matters even better, he loved that her mini-me was almost a replica of her. Having the two ladies in his life has made him want to speed up his plans.

He rested his eyes on the safety of the woman he was growing to love. A sexual thought was replaced with something stronger. Hours later, she wakes up, and the sun has already gone down. Javier is up, and she hears Kimmie giggling in the bathroom. She gets up and walks inside to find Javier sitting on the toilet's lid with Kimmie putting blush and eyeshadow all over his face.

Javier asked. "I pray you don't mind."

Then my mom replied, "She made you put this on?"

Javier quipped, "She got into your makeup, and I think I startled her, so I said she could put it on me."

"Kimmie. You got into mommy's makeup?" Kimmie looks down and away from her mom. Javier says, "She was just messing around. I wanted to show her how to put it on correctly. So I put a little on her lips and eyes and said she could try to do the same on my face."

"So you are the reason my daughter is in here looking like a beauty queen?"

"Guilty," he replies jokingly.

"You both ready to wash that off your faces?"

"Actually, I don't think we are done just yet."

"Oh, what else are you going to let her do?"

"Not sure, but she has been giggling since we've been at it. I enjoy seeing her eyes light up."

"Well, we have to go to the store. I need a few things for dinner."

"You can go, and I can stay here and wash up after. I don't mind–I mean, if you are comfortable with that of course?"

"Oh, yeah, I should be back real quick. The store is around the corner, and I need only a few things. Be about twenty minutes."

"Yeah, that's fine. I will have everything cleaned up by then. No problem."

Kristina disappears from the door jamb. Kimmie keeps drawing lines of color on Javier's face. Javier reciprocates with mascara and asks Kimmie to open her eyes as he applies it. She looked like a doll when he was finished. He did surprisingly well putting on makeup. He picks her up so she can see the look in the mirror.

"What do you think, my Doll baby? Do you like it?"

She nods her head and says, "Yes. I like it."

He puts her on the floor and says, "Good, you look gorgeous. Let's wash your face so your mom can have you all cleaned up for when she gets back." He looks for a rag and finds a few in a closet. He puts the rag underwater and lets it run from cold to warm. He puts a very little bit of soap on the rag and brings it toward her face.

Only Kimmie decides to push the rag away. "No, I don't want to wash it off."

"Your mom wants you to clean your face. So I have to take it off."

No, I don't want to take it off.

"Okay, what if I told you you could put on a dress and take a picture? Then I would have to wipe it off and put on your clothes. Do you want to play dress-up?"

"Okay!" She goes to her room and takes out a dress she likes. She comes back to the bathroom with the dress and says, "I want this dress."

"Okay, let me help you put it on." Javier takes her shirt off and removes her pants. He picks up the dress and asks her, "Okay, lift your arms." Kimmie lifts her arms up, and the door opens.

"Yo man, what the hell are you doing?" shouts Gerald.

"I was just playing with Kimmie. Who are you?" replied Javier.

"That's my daughter. Where is her mother?"

"She went to the store; she should be back shortly."

"I was just putting her dress on because we were just playing."

"Do you play with your own daughter like this?"

He clears his throat, "I actually don't have children yet, but I plan to have a gorgeous little girl like yours."

"Bro, I don't know how I feel right now, but I can tell you it ain't good. Joy, come here, go put your clothes back on."

"The ones she just had on are right here, I was just helping–"

"Shut up. I don't need you to say anything. Baby, go get you some clothes on. Mommy's friend and I need to have a conversation."

Kristina walks in the door and sees Kimmie dressed in her underwear. She runs toward the bathroom after hearing a large crash. "What the hell? Stop it!"

She sees that Gerald gave Javier a busted lip, and his arm was retracting for a second hit. Before he could stop his arm from swinging forward, Javier ducks and scoots around to behind Kristina. "Baby, will you tell him I am your friend? And it doesn't look like what he thinks."

"What is going on, and why are you here?"

"I got a call, and I thought to stop by. I told you I would come if I could before leaving."

"Yeah, but you also said you would call first. You never come, so why would you come today?"

"Honestly, my mom saw you two love birds walking down the street with my daughter. I don't like my daughter around another man that I don't know. I certainly don't want her sitting on his neck."

He continues to say, "Then I got here, and I didn't see your car, but I heard her giggling. So I used my key in case you left her at home or something. Crazy shit like that happens. I see this man over here with my daughter, painted up and her naked."

"She wasn't naked, Bro. She was changing into her dress to take a picture. We did our faces, and I wanted her mom to have the picture."

"Kristina, please tell me you don't think this is cool?"

"Well, I saw the two of them playing before I went to the store. So I knew that the two of them were playing with makeup and stuff. Kristina loves to play dress-up. I am sure all of this is a big misunderstanding. Can we talk for a minute outside?"

Javier backs up from the door and goes into Kristina's bedroom. Kimmie reappears wearing a mismatched top and bottoms. "Thanks, baby. Now go get your shoes."

"Kristina, you lost your damn mind. And there ain't no way I am going to allow her to stay here in this confusion. You can call the cops if you want to, but I am leaving with my daughter."

"Don't you think you are overreacting?"

"Do you hear yourself? I pray the sex is really good because that is the only thing that would make a woman act like this. Yo, something is wrong with you. And I don't care how you fix it, but she ain't going to be here for it. Just call my mom if you need to speak to her. I am done with you."

"Gerald, you can't just keep taking her because we don't agree. I have a right to move on and have a man. I don't have to tell you what I am doing or explain my life to you anymore!"

"This isn't about you! If that is what you heard, you are so lost. You ditzy. My issue is that you got some random dude around my daughter who I don't know. She was in her underwear when I came, Kristina. For real, you don't think that is odd?"

"Do you really think he was going to try something with her? She is almost two years old. What man would do that, honestly? We had such a good day today, and this is the first time that they have really spent time together."

"And in one day, you left him alone with our daughter, and I find her naked. You cool with that?"

"Again, I think you need to calm down."

"You need to back away from me because I don't trust myself. I am leaving." He calls out to me, "Joy, let's go!" Out of the room, I run with my clothes, shoes, and backpack on. "Go tell Mommy you will see her later." I came up to my mother to give her a hug, and she hugged me back. "Bye, Kimmie. I will be by to see you later today."

"No, don't come today. Come tomorrow or something. In fact, take the week and figure it out. I am not paying for anything else up in here. I said I would help you, but clearly you don't need my help no more. She can stay with me. She won't live here no more."

"You can't do that."

"Watch me." He picks up his daughter and heads out the door. A few moments later, Javier comes out of the room. "Look, Babe; I don't know what just happened."

"Can you tell me why my daughter was walking around in her underwear?"

"Yes, I was trying to wipe the makeup off her face. She pushed my hand and said she didn't want to take it off. I said if she wanted to put on a dress and take a picture, she could, then we would have to take off the makeup and put her same clothes on."

"Now, why would you do that?"

"I was just trying to keep her from crying. She wanted to wear a dress. I was going to take a picture so you can see what fun we had, and that was it. It was nothing weird. If she were my daughter, I would have done the same thing, and no one would be weirded out like this."

"Javier, but she is not your daughter!"

"Yeah, but aren't we getting serious? I love you. I want to be with you and be a father to Kimmie. I am here. I was trying to play and do the girl dad stuff."

"I know, but this, this doesn't feel right."

"You know me. We have been dating for months now. I have never done anything that would hint at something like that, and you know that. Your ex doesn't know me, and he doesn't know us. Don't base your opinion on what he just said. Trust how I have treated you and what you've seen me do these past few months."

He goes to hug my mother and reassures her, "I love you. Did you hear me say that?"

Kristina replies, "Yes, I heard you say that. I love you too." She kisses him, and they both share a moment until Javier winces from the pain on the left side of his face. "Oh, Baby, you need an ice pack."

"Yeah, he swung while I still had the dress in my hand, and I was unprepared. I wasn't trying to fight in front of no baby, you know?"

"Yeah, I can understand." She grabs him a bag of veggies from the fridge and places it on his face. He smiles and nods to say thanks.

It wasn't a week later that Kristina got papers in the mail for an upcoming emergency custody hearing. She read over the paperwork, "Really, Gerald? You are suing me for child support and primary custody?" She read the letter mesmerized and a bit confused about what to do. She had no money and no way of taking care of herself. She was stuck!

Javier saw her reading the letter and asked, "What can I do? How can I help? My bad, Babe."

"It's cool; I will figure it out."

"No, we will figure it out. We are becoming a family whether your ex likes it or not. He can't control how you live your life. If you need to move in with me, let's do it."

"I don't want to rush what we are building because Gerald is scared for me to move on. That is not fair to you or our relationship."

"It's not a rush. If he pulls the plug on your money, and now you have to pay him, what are you going to do? You got your test coming up. I told you I would help."

"I don't really know about this."

"Just trust me. I can do this, and I want to do it for you. Custody battles can be messy and expensive. Don't you need a lawyer?"

"I didn't even think of that."

"Trust me, you should get a lawyer."

"With what money?"

"I can help."

"I really do appreciate you. I don't know what's happening, but I am so glad you are here." She kisses him, and they work on a plan to address the changes on the horizon.

It was a crazy time at the custody hearing. Against Javier's judgment, Kristina didn't get a lawyer. She got the bill and felt it would be money ill spent. She thought leaning on the truth was enough. Married people share custody. Gerald is on the road working overnights, so my mom should be the primary parent.

She said to herself, "This is a closed case. No one can better provide for her than her mother and father. He is busy on the road except for some weekends and two days out of the week sometimes. That is not enough time to care for our daughter."

Javier replies, "I know and see what you are thinking. But how can you be sure that is all the judge will look at? I am sure your ex is going to pull out your work history and me."

"There are too many women getting child support without a job. Hell, that is what child support is for. To help support the child. He has been doing it this long; why would it be a problem now?"

"People get funny."

"I am going to be fine. I am sure the judge will see through his jealousy, and everything will be cool. I can say I have a place to stay and that I am finishing my exam. It's not like I can't make money, Javier."

"Okay," he says reluctantly, "If this is how you feel. I will support you."

She thanks him and heads out the door to attend court. When she arrives, my mom is unsure of where to park, so after ten minutes of looking for a spot, she parks and walks briskly through the court doors. There is a long line of people already waiting. She goes to the check-in counter and speaks with the administrator, who tells her, "The other party is here; they will call our case shortly."

She was shuffled to one side of the court, awaiting her case number to be called. After what seemed like twenty minutes, their case number was called. My mom and Gerald responded and approached their respective sides of the bench to speak on the matter.

"Your Honor, I am here today seeking primary custody from my ex-wife because she is dating a pedophile."

"Are you crazy, Gerald? No, I am not dating a pedophile." The Judge breaks up the argument before it ensues, further: "Hey, you both are in my court, and you will not speak to each other. Got it?"

Kristina replies, "Yes, sorry."

"Please continue," replies the Judge.

"I went by the house on October 10th, and my daughter was hemmed up in the bathroom, with makeup on her face, no shirt, no pants. When I saw her with her mother's boyfriend, I tried to stay calm."

"Okay, does that sound correct, Mrs. James?"

"Your Honor, the part he left out. He was fighting with Javier when I came into the bathroom. Our daughter was in the hallway changing. And yes, the two of them were playing dress up and using makeup. But there was nothing happening."

"Your Honor, how can she be sure if she wasn't there?"

"Were you there while they were playing?" asks the judge.

"I was asleep on the couch at first, but I woke up and watched them paint on each other's faces. They were both laughing and having a good time. Even he knows they were playing. When he came to the house unannounced, he said she was giggling, and that's what made him come inside."

"Your honor, I came inside because I thought she had left her there alone. I didn't see her car out front."

"Is this true, Mrs. James? Were you gone when he arrived?"

"Yes, I rode to the store to get a few things for dinner. I was only gone about fifteen minutes. It wasn't long at all. I did tell Javier, my boyfriend, to clean up everything before I got back. So he just walked in at a bad time."

"Mr. James, is there anything else you want to tell me so that I can consider this petition?"

"She doesn't have a place to live, your Honor, or an income. I was paying for all the bills at the house to help in addition to my child support so our daughter would be good, but now that she is in a new relationship. Now, I really don't feel she is safe, so I don't see why I should pay for her living anymore if my daughter is with me. Our daughter can stay with me in a safer environment with the support of my mother, who is home full-time, and she is here today." Gerald points to his mother sitting behind him.

"Mrs. James, do you have an income or a place to live if the lease to this apartment is no longer an option?"

"Yes, my boyfriend has a place that we will stay in together. I am currently in school and will be taking my medical coding exam next week. So I will have employment. Infinity HIM Medical School helps with prospective job placement."

"You mean to tell me you are going to move into the house with the pedophile?"

"Mr. James, direct your questions to me."

"Yes, Judge, of course. Sorry. " Gerald is clearly upset. He looks down; his leg starts to shake a little.

"Mrs. James, how long have you known your boyfriend?"

"A few months dating, your Honor. But we met last year."

"Okay, so this is a long-term relationship?"

Gerald raises his hand. The judge sees his hand and calls on him, "Your Honor, this is the same man that broke up our marriage several months back, almost a year now. He is the man I caught on camera sleeping with my wife."

"Mrs. James, is this true?"

"Your honor,"

"Answer the question, Mrs. James."

"Yes."

"Do you have anything else for me to hear?"

"Your honor, I can take care of my baby. I am a good mother."

My dad interjects, "Your Honor, a few months ago, she left our two-year-old with her grandmother, who could barely walk or stay alert. She didn't know our daughter was there because Kristina snuck out the door to see this same guy. I don't care who she dates, but her relationship with him is making me question her ability to put our daughter's needs first. My mother had to call me to go and get our child, and I called off driving trucks to see about her."

He seems to not breathe as he continues to say, "She was there with a loaded diaper. She had a rash, and her sick mother was asleep the whole time–completely unaware of where Kristina had gone or that our daughter was there. She could have turned the stove on or anything! I came and picked her up and kept her with me for about two weeks. She never called to complain or demand I bring her back at all."

"Judge, he works all the time and is never home. He is only home two days out of the week and pops up on weekends to spy on me," retorts Kristina.

"Excuse me, Mrs. James. Let's be clear. Did you leave your daughter with your grandmother, who you knew couldn't provide for her?"

"Judge, she was playing, and she would be fine. I was only around the corner. I didn't even know my boyfriend would show up; we hadn't seen each other for months prior to that."

"Okay, I think I have heard enough. Give me a moment to deliberate, and I will be back with my order."

It wasn't long before the order was read, and Gerald left smiling from ear to ear. Kristina was ordered to pay $97 a week for support, and she would get supervised visitation until her living conditions changed. Kristina went out heartbroken. The case didn't go as planned in the slightest bit. She felt it was highly unfair and was based on a bias the judge had and not the honest facts.

My mom wasn't a perfect mother, but she deserved to make mistakes. No mother got it all right, and she admitted to her mistakes, but for her to be judged seemed harsh to her. She cried that night with Javier by her side while explaining her situation to him. He assured her everything was fine and she had nothing to worry about.

Javier saw how hard it was for my mom the next few days and knew she couldn't take her exam until her mind was cleared. He took her on a three-day vacation in Vegas. He wanted her to feel light, fun, appreciated, and loved.

The two of them enjoyed attending parties, going to clubs, and eating great food. Seeing the bright lights made her feel alive. She felt empowered and felt the world could indeed be theirs. Going up into the sky on that late night and seeing the lights from high off the ground made her heart race, but also proved she was alive.

"If you can see yourself somewhere, Kristina,

you can do it. You don't have to be fake; you can acknowledge when something hurts. But don't let this break you. You are a diamond, beautiful and powerful. There is nothing you cannot do."

He kisses my mom and squeezes her hand. She accepts the encouragement while she takes in the lights and skyline. It is energizing. She is ready to head home, not as the same woman but as one who has seen people using whatever they have to make money on the streets and performing on stages. She likes sitting by the pool and ordering drinks without a care in the world.

She wanted to be free and believed even more now in what medical coding could do for her. She was ready to take the test because she could see the importance of why she needed to pass it. She wanted to live on her own terms. Although she appreciated the olive branch from Javier, she wanted to prove herself independently.

She didn't want to rely heavily on him to pay her way or to look like a failure to Gerald. Although the relationship with Javier is much different, her desire for herself is the same. She wants independence! She needed this shift in her life. She saw that her apartment loss was a blessing that helped push her toward her ambitious drive and goal.

My mom saw that her having a break from me was the right thing also to happen. She needed to focus, and playing a quasi-housewife did not help her reach her goal. She needed to cut all the ties from her past to move forward. I was the only link to her past, and she wanted to keep things that way.

She knew that on that day, she had been reborn. Javier took Mom to Vegas to help shake off her stress. When she returned with him, she was even more focused, encouraged, empowered, and ready to accomplish whatever she set out to do.

The plane ride was peaceful even though it bumped around like the Magic School Bus in the air. The drop in altitude made my mom's ears feel like they were turning inside out. They both were relieved when they landed. Before hitting the ground, her mind was preoccupied with needing to get her own place and the steps she would take.

Mom took her medical coding exams the same week and passed them all with flying colors. When my dad's lease was up, he promptly turned off the lights and removed the water from his name. Following suit, the complex sent her a friendly letter stating its intention to vacate the apartment immediately.

She knew the day was coming, but it still felt like a punch to her gut when she read the words. It didn't stir up fear like before in her belly, but motivation. My mom called every job hiring and submitted nearly ten applications a day for a week. Javier was such a great support, and the candlelight dinners, bubble baths, and late nights made her feel like she was on top of the world. She couldn't have been happier.

But then it happened. My mother got the job she wanted the most! She had it all: the man, the job, and now the money was on its way. All that was missing was her baby. She thought of challenging the judge's order now that she was doing well, but her good sense said to wait until she got her own place.

She left that part out of the story. She didn't tell Javier that she planned to move out so she could get custody of her daughter. Although she wasn't a mother who instantly gravitated to her daughter, the weeks without her were like a knife through the stomach. She didn't want to live like this, she needed her daughter.

My mom was waiting for her first check to come in the mail because they were old school, and direct deposit didn't kick in until her second check. She kept checking the mail, looking for it. One day, the mail came, and she knew she would find something worth smiling about amongst the few envelopes. She got the stack of mail, and without thinking, she opened the first one, assuming it was for her. The other days, it was nothing more than mailers and coupons sent to every mailbox for advertising.

She opened the letter inside, thinking it would be a check, but it was a letter from the courts. She looked at the petitioner and respondent, but the lines didn't read her name or her ex-husband's. It was made out to Shamicka Johnson vs Javier Santos. She read it again to be sure it wasn't a typo.

She checked the front, and the letter was written to Javier. She read the complaint, and her mouth dropped. She couldn't believe what she was reading. It was a slap in the face that instantly brought tears.

She went on a rampage throughout the house, looking for any sightings of mail. She checked every kitchen drawer, sock drawer, and even his closet. It wasn't until she opened a drawer in his bathroom and looked underneath to find a basket with a waterproof bag full of letters. She read writings that described Javier Santos vs. Shondra Jackson, Javier Santos vs. Denise Danner, and Jasmine Jacobs.

She read letter after letter confirming her worst fear and Gerald's suspicion. He was accused of having inappropriate relationships with children under five. Without saying anything, through tears, she started to pack all of her things into a single suitcase.

My mother grabbed the new computer he bought for her, the clothes, and everything her eyes laid on that was hers before she ran up out of the house. She was lying with the lion and had no idea. She didn't realize until that moment how much danger her daughter could have been in with her relationship choice. It scared her that she could have been another case in a bathroom drawer or under the sink.

She would never admit it to Gerald, but she also had to find somewhere to go. She had no one else to call because she and Jasmine had stopped being friends months back. She didn't like Kristina's mood and inability to go places. She wanted to have fun. But tonight, she could really use her help.

She called Jasmine, and to her surprise, she picked up. Something she hadn't done in months. My mom spoke and said, "Hey, Jasmine."

"Hey, how you been?"

"I could be better."

"You calling me because you need a babysitter again?"

Kristina couldn't respond before she burst into tears. "No, I just-just–"

"Okay, where are you? And what are you doing right now?"

"I am walking down the street with a suitcase headed to my grandmother's house. I just didn't want to be at Javier's place right now. I swear I have my crap together, Jasmine."

"Okay, let me come pick you up."

My mother puts up no contest. She walks to the corner to wait for her long-lost friend to arrive. Jasmine pulls up about thirty minutes later and my mother is happy to see her. She put her things in the trunk and got in.

"Dang girl, did you move into a mini apartment?"

"Well, I got kicked out of my apartment a few weeks ago."

"Okay, I figured something like that would happen when you quit."

"It wasn't because of what you think. I lost custody of Kimmie."

"Wait, what?"

"What the hell did you do to lose custody of your child?"

"The guy I met at the club, Javier, we've been getting close. I had him over, and Gerald came by while he was there."

"Okay, I'm still not seeing an issue."

"He found Javier playing dress up with Kimmie."

"Okay, what am I missing?"

"She was dressed in her underwear, and he undressed her to put a dress on her. She was playing in my makeup and he wanted to play with her so I didn't get mad."

"So you let a grown man–who wasn't your daughter's father, play dress, take her clothes off, and put makeup on her face?"

"See, I know this sounds bad. Please don't judge me. I am going through a lot right now. But it was innocent."

"Girl, you lost your dang mind. You never should be okay with a man putting any kind of makeup on his face or undressing your daughter. Please tell me y'all broke up today?"

She shook her head no. And Jasmine jumped at the response, "So you stayed with him? What could he have said to make you be okay with your daughter having her face made up and her walking around naked?"

"I know it sounds bad, but you had to have been there. She was holding her arms up to have her dress put on. Kimmie was so sweet playing with Javier, and he never gave the impression it was anything more than him wanting to be a girl dad."

"Did Gerald beat the breaks off of him when he saw that?"

"He tried to. I came into the bathroom when the fight started and broke it up. But he took her that day, and we went to court. The short answer is that he won full custody, and I got stuck paying child support. I even have supervised visitations until I moved out from my boyfriend's place."

"Wait, you were in a relationship with a pedophile?"

"Come on, Jasmine, this is already hard."

"But if this is the truth, you need to face this.

What are you going to do?"

"I broke up with him."

"Wait, so what convinced you he was a pedo-phile? Because you said earlier–"

"I was in his mail looking for my paycheck. I started a job a few weeks back, so I thought the mail was my check. I opened it up, and I saw that he had a case pending against him for pedophilia against a minor under five."

"Wait, so he was convicted?"

"I searched his whole apartment because it was a notice for him to respond. I thought he would have another letter to say when this case started, but I found three other cases he had against him instead. I want to look him up and see if he has any convic-tions, but I am scared to check. I am just so mad at myself that I didn't see it coming."

"Girl, you need to check this right now." Kristina started searching the online registry and Jasmine continues to say. "I mean, you couldn't know this man was sick like this. You can't blame yourself, Kristina." My mom was there crying while she explained all that she was thinking and how guilty she looked and felt. If Gerald had had these details, he would have judiciously nailed her to the wall and maybe got her into serious trouble.

Kristina, breathes out and says, "No, he is not registered on the sex offenders list. It still pains me that I had him around my daughter, I would have just thrown up in my mouth if something hap-pened. He gave no signs of something like this. I had no idea."

"Let's get home and take a moment to relax.

I do have some company so if you cool with that, I can bring you around my place."

"Yeah, any place is better than my mom's." The girls drive in silence. Kristina looks out the window, dumbfounded at everything that is lost in a blink of an eye. Things were so good with Javier; how could this be true, she thought. She wanted to deny it, but she had four cases to prove this man was doing something inappropriate with girls, and she lost interest in finding out what. She was grateful that Gerald had custody because he likely saved her from something she had no idea was coming her way.

They arrive at Jasmine's house and get out of the car. Jasmine opens the door and hollers out, "Bay, I'm back. Don't come out here. I've got company." You could hear his footsteps retreat back to the room, and the door closed shut. A few moments later, a man wearing basketball shorts and a t-shirt emerged from the room. "Hey, thanks for the heads up." He kisses Jasmine on the back of the neck and sits on the couch.

"Hey, don't I recognize you?"

Kristina shakes her head no. She doesn't remember him from anywhere that comes to mind. But he rubs his chin, tilts his head to the side, and replies, "No, no, I remember you. Didn't you come to the club with Jasmine back in the day?"

"Yeah, it's been like a year. I only came like twice. You sure it was me?"

"Yeah, it was you. That night, you were tripped by Oh Boy and dropped everything on the floor. You remember that night?"

"No, actually, only parts of it. But what you mean tripped me?"

"You know that dude tripped you, right? I saw him take your ID and stuff from the floor. I tried to tell you when I pulled you aside, but he wouldn't let me talk to you."

"Oh, I thought you just wanted–"

"Nah, I wasn't interested—no disrespect, but you're not my type. Shondra dated him for a bit, and the guy is weird. He likes children a little too much, and that made her uncomfortable. She didn't tell me what he did, but it must have been bad enough she wanted to press charges. He keeps

pushing the date back and getting things resched-
uled for one reason or another."

"Really?"

"Yeah, I'm sure he will end up paying her
some money. The guy is loaded from insurance
money. If he didn't try nothing, I am sure she will
take the money. I think the dude is more strange
than a pedophile, from what she told me. Do you
dodge one when you got away from him."

"No, she didn't. She dated him," replied Jasmine.

"No, tell me you didn't. You don't have a little
girl, do you?" Kristina nodded her head yes, and his
mouth dropped.

Jasmine jumped in and said, "I think her
dad prevented anything too crazy. Who would have
thought he was into toddlers that way? The dude
sounds weird, but that doesn't mean he is a pedophile. Inappropriate, yeah. I don't think a grown
man should take off any girl's clothes unless they are
the ambulance or doctor or something."

"I would have tried to take his head off. No
questions asked."

"Her dad did; I had to break up the fight."

"So y'all broke up over that?"

"I really don't want to talk about this anymore. Jasmine, do you have something to eat?"
Kristina gets up from the couch and enters the
kitchen while Jasmine and the man gossip about her
life decisions. She felt foolish inside the kitchen and
regretted going there. But she would feel that crummy no matter where she went. She messed up, and

now, to know this made her boil.

The room began to circle, and my mom hurried to drink water to keep her balance. The little food she ate wasn't enough to fill her up, but she lost her appetite. She needed to rest, but she wanted to hide out in the kitchen for as long as possible to avoid their questions and judging eyes. She had already judged herself and didn't need more thoughts. Her plan was to keep working, get her own place with her next check, and start over.

Back at Gerald's place, life was a challenge. Gerald's mother helped every day to care for me, her granddaughter. She enjoyed spending time with me and seeing me grow. She always wanted a close relationship with her grandchildren, but I was more than she had bargained for. Grandma never complained, but she did feel drained on some days.

Gerald was good at helping whenever he was home, but he was also getting burned out on the road. Working double shifts and picking up whenever someone couldn't make it were getting old. He wanted to be home more and desperately wanted to raise me.

He enjoyed our kiddie adventures at the park and the local indoor playhouses. I enjoyed jumping around for what seemed like hours and playing in the indoor sandbox. I naturally liked science and things related to pouring a substance from one object into another.

My dad liked watching me play in different costumes. He would joke and say that I would make a good doctor or a scientist someday. I've always wanted to make something that involved mixing and holding stuff in my hands. Dad knew then I would be using my brain and hands. He smiled while he cleaned up my mess.

My dad's mother was an elegant woman; she taught me invaluable skills. I learned how to pick up my mess, study hard, and put forth my best effort even when things got complicated. Life was different for her, but it was a reasonable adjustment from outsiders. I was doing preschool activities daily with my grandmother, and my speech improved quickly. I was speaking full sentences by my third birthday, and my growth continued.

My life was set for the next two years until, one day, my grandmother got a call. She dropped her soft and friendly tone, and her eyes grew serious. Looking on as a five-year-old, I wasn't sure of what was happening, but I knew it wasn't good. Grandma got off the phone and said, "Come on, we have to go. Please put on your shoes quickly."

My grandmother and I rushed out of the door and got into the car. Uncertain about where we were going, I asked, "Grandma, is everything okay?"

"It will be a little bit. Just give grandma a minute to think, okay? But I am fine." My grandmother was quiet on the ride, and she looked out the window to pass the time. We arrived at the hospital a short time later and parked.

"Grandma, why are we at the hospital? Is somebody hurt?"

"Yes, no, I mean, yes, we are at the hospital, but he is fine."

"Who is hurt?" Grandma was walking quickly into the hospital, and my feet felt like Squidworth as I walked in behind her. She was focused on getting to the desk, and my small talk was put on hold. She welcomed the silence, and I didn't fight her so she could focus on whoever it was we were going to see. I could tell she was worried about the outcome but was praying behind her silence for the best.

"Hi Ma'am, how can I help you?"

"Yes, I am here looking for my son, Gerald James."
"Yes, he is here. Do you have an ID?" She handed over her ID, and then we went to see my dad. We enter the room, and he is awake, awaiting our presence. Dad greets us, saying, "Hey, mom. You didn't have to come down here. I am doing alright. Just a few broken bones, but I am fine, honestly."

He looks at me and says, "Hey, Joy. How was school?"

"It was good, Dad. How did you get into the hospital?" I asked as I gave him a hug.

"Dad got into an accident today on the truck, but I am more than fine. I just have to take it easy to heal, and I will be fine."

"Okay, so when can you leave the hospital? Do you have to stay here to heal?"

"No, I am sure I will be going home today or tomorrow. They are just running some tests."

"Baby, you know if you need me to take care of everything, that is no problem."

"I know, Mom. I enjoy helping with what I can, and I plan to get back into my routine soon enough."

The three of us exchange jokes, and everyone's spirit stays high. It was good that Dad had us in the hospital with him because that meant we stopped our life for him like he had always done for us. It is the simple things that make a big difference.

He was grateful for his family.

The next few days at the hospital were hard on his body, but he was ready to go home and start the healing process. But there was a catch: Dad had to pay his medical bills. He had insurance but wasn't sure of all the details. He planned to have a conversation with his dad when he returned.

He dreaded the conversation because any money conversation seemed to stress Granddad out. He was under a lot of pressure during COVID-19 to move products with limited drivers, no shipment to pick up when they arrived, and the miles with gas prices going berserk has not been easy. The best employee my grandfather had was my dad. My dad was the only one who did not need time off due to Covid.

Grandad knew his son was due for some time off, but he couldn't lose him. My dad was the anchor next to Grandpa to keep the company afloat. Being so busy and having to thin out the company so much to make a profit, he did have to cut some corners. One of the corners was reducing coverage.

Gerald returned home with a sling, bandages over his damaged rib cage, and a knee brace. I thought he looked like a character from television, and I enjoyed bringing him food and drinks while he was on the couch. I had no idea how hard it was for him to sit at home when he knew his dad needed him.

But he couldn't avoid having this conversation with him because the hospital kept pressing on the bill. So he rings his dad's phone while he is on the road. Grandpa picks up, but his mood is not great. He got some bad news about dropping a load off and is trying to breathe through it so he doesn't start yelling.

"Hello, Son, how are you feeling?"

"Considering everything good, Dad. How are things for you?"

"Going. I will figure it out. So what did the doctors say?"

"I will be out for several weeks. I damaged some ribs. And some issues with my knee and right arm."

"Dang, Son. This couldn't have come at a worse time. I really could use your help out here, but your healing is first."

"Yeah, but you know when I can come back, I will be there."

"Yes, Son, I know that."

"But Dad, I got to ask you something. The hospital has been calling me and asking about insurance details to clear my debts with them. Do you know who I should call to pick up the balance?"

"Well, Son, I don't really handle all the details like that. But I think we have only one company. I had reduced the coverage because we hadn't had a serious accident in years. I felt like going down in coverage was a good thing. So whatever the insurance covers should cover all your bills."

"It hasn't. I am still getting some pretty high bills, and I don't have it."

"Well, we don't have it either. So maybe you can work something out with the hospital or sue the other driver?"

"Dad, this accident was my fault. There is no

one to sue. I fell asleep because I told you I needed to rest."

"So you are blaming me?"

"No, this is on the company, not you."

"Look, we are working, Gerald. We don't get to take days off if that means missing a load. I drive just as much as you, and I am stressed, too. But I am not getting into wrecks. This is not our fault. I never told you not to sleep; you know you should."

"But you pushed for deadlines and kept adding dates, Dad. I cannot satisfy your demands, and neither can my sleeping schedule. I haven't had a real day off in years. Even when I am home, I make local deliveries."

"But, son, you needed the money the same as I do. You have a daughter to think about and school."

"Yeah, Dad. I cannot eat these hospital bills."

"So you are going to throw them on my lap?"

"Dad, it is the company's lap."

"Well, how do you think the company is doing with you being out?"

"Um–"

"Son, we are barely surviving. I need you to do the best you can so I can keep the business afloat. I am doing all of this for you. When I am dead and gone, this will be yours."

"Dad, I understand that. But I cannot pay for these medical bills. This isn't fair. We need to come up with something to make this right."

"Look, I gotta go." The men hang up with a less-than-ideal "goodbye." My dad hated confronting his dad because he knew this wasn't easy for both of them. His mom came into the room and asked, "So, how did it go?"

"Dad doesn't have the money, Mom. What do I do? Let this accident tear up my credit?"

"Naw, you can't do that. You need good credit to get anything. If you still want to buy the house, you can't let your credit fall, Son."

"You are going to have to think of something else."

"Do you really think the company is doing as badly as Dad thinks? You know how he can be with money."

"Yeah, your father is resourceful but isn't a liar. I cannot help you go after your father, but I know you have to do what is best for you, too. I just hate that money is becoming what it is."

"I know, Mom. I am sorry you are put in between us like this."

"Well, right now, there is nothing to say that I am in between. Let's just pray it stays that way."

She gives him a hug and a kiss and then exits the room. Gerald's phone rings, and he answers, "Hello?"

"Hi, this is Frontier Global Insurance. I wanted to update you on your claim."

"Yes, I also have some medical bills. Do you

think you can add them to the claim?”

"Well, upon further review, we understand this accident occurred because you fell asleep at the wheel. We are reimbursing for your comprehension collision claim, but your medical claim has been denied.”

"Denied?”

"Yes, we read the police report and checked your rest logs. Based on that, we will not be able to honor your medical claim.”

"This is bull–” his mother comes into the room and stops him before he can finish his sentence. She grabs the phone and says, "Thank you for your time. Have a wonderful day.”

Grandma gives my dad a scolding look and asks him, "What is wrong with you? Don't lose your temper like that! Kimberly could hear you. Now, do you want to tell me what is going on?"

"That was the insurance company, Mom. They just said they are not going to pay out on the medical claim."

"Can they do that?"

"They can, I guess. I will look into it. But I called Dad, too. He was saying he couldn't help with the medical bills either. I know I didn't follow all the rules, but right now, none of the drivers are. We are working crazy hours, and with Covid, people are calling in all the time."

"Yeah, no one could have predicted this storm coming our way."

"But Mom, if Dad can't help me with the bills, I will have to do something I don't want to do."

"What do you mean?"

"I will have to sue the company. I cannot afford the bills. I know Kimmie and I are supposed to get a house soon. I cannot mess up my credit. Now is the best time to get a house."

"Yeah, I hear you, but son, don't you think you are being too critical of this situation? Are you sure there is nothing else you can do instead of suing your father? Maybe there is a program at the hospital that can pay down the debt."

"With the insurance programs we have, we are liable for 50% of our medical bills. I don't have $50,000 lying around for a medical expense that is honestly not my fault. I told Dad I needed to rest–but he wasn't hearing me. Now, I am broken up, can't drive, and am looking at losing my house deposit. Tell me–is that fair?"

"Son, life is not fair. I cannot tell you what to do. I would love to see you and Kimberly in your own home because I know how hard you have been working. You deserve this house. You honestly do. Just think of a way to get it done that doesn't hurt your father if you can. He is really under pressure, too. He would never have you work all these hours if it weren't necessary."

"Mom, I have been flexible. I just can't bend on this." She pats him on the shoulder and replies, "I know, Son." She walks away in silence. Gerald is left sitting on the couch, stunned by how he can make sense of suing his father. Why did life have to get so complicated? How come it had to come to this at all? This was what insurance was for, after all.

The ordeal seemed unfair to the family, but the fiscal storm was there, and they had no choice but to go through it. My dad's father got news of the filing while at home for a brief few hours before setting off to another job. It was hard for Grandad not to walk up to my dad and slap the spit out of his mouth, but he knew that would solve nothing.

He left out of the house and didn't say a word to my dad. Dad was uncomfortable sitting on the couch his dad bought, knowing he would have to sue him. But it wasn't his father he was suing; it was the company. My dad figured he would only be forced to move money around that he likely had but didn't want to pay out in this way.

My dad and grandpa were between a rock and a hard place. The fire between the two of them singed the heart of Grandma every time they had a blowup. She tried to keep the peace, and as the accident suit grew near, the two of them became more and more combative with each other, mostly in words.

Dinner time was spent with my grandparents eating first, and my dad and I would eat after them. It was painful for both of us to live through their war because I missed my grandfather. He always had good jokes to tell at dinner time. My dad stopped joking when Granddaddy got notice of the suit and put him on leave without pay. He also refused to pay the fine he got for not making the necessary stops and violating DOT (Department of Transportation) laws.

My dad was furious and thought this was an unreasonable hardball move, so after not being able to take any more games, he confronted my grandpa in a neutral space. "Hey, Dad, can we talk?"

"You mean like how we should have before you slapped a suit against me, Son?"

"Come on, Dad, you know this isn't about us. Why are you being so petty about this? This is my issue with the company and not you personally. If I was working anywhere else and I got injured on the job, it would be a covered expense, and you know it."

"But Son, right now just isn't the time for me to do that. The business cannot afford a hit like this, and you don't care."

"Dad, I work around the clock for this company, and you know it. Anything you have asked me to do, I have done–and I don't complain. This was not an easy decision for me, and you know this. I don't want to sue you, Dad, but we had a conversation, and you don't see that this is between the company and me, not you and I."

"That is where you are wrong, Gerald. I built this company, and sadly, I built it for you–for us. How can you be so selfish and think this is the right way to handle this? I will never understand. You could call into question everything I have built and for what? Because of one bill, Gerald?"

"Dad, this is not a petty thing. I cannot pay fifty thousand dollars on medical bills."

"You can't, or you won't?"

"I am not."

"That is selfish. You have the money. I once gave you seventeen thousand dollars, and I didn't demand nothing from you when you couldn't come up with the money on your own."

"Dad, you told me immediately THAT I had to work for you and pay off the debt, which I did more than two times over. I have given up my life for this company. I am not complaining, but I am sacrificing the same as you. I just can't give my house money to the business."

"Even though this is your business? And you live with me."

I pay bills here too, Dad. I pay a third of all the expenses even though I am never here. I give Mom money every week to take care of Kimmie, and you know that, Dad. I am not abusing either one of you. I have earned everything I have, and you have made sure of that. It is unfair to ask me to give up on my future house because you say the business needs to come first."

"Son, do you doubt me?"

"No, Dad, I don't. But I cannot bail out the company; I need to provide for my daughter. "

"Well, I pray you know what you are doing." My Granddad put his hat on slowly and walked out the door. The last words from him rang in my dad's ears long after the exit. He couldn't shake the words and began to question if he was doing the right thing. What if the company was really struggling?

Yes, my dad knew the company could be in trouble even before the accident, but how much trouble, he questioned. Why was Granddad being so overly combative? Was the company on the verge of collapse? Could it be that Granddad's pride kept him from telling anyone the truth about the business?

Granddad went out the door and slowly got into his company truck. The truck he loved for years that was the bridge to help my dad get married and the lifeboat to provide for his family. Now is the catalyst for the fallout between him and his son.

He thought how can a vehicle have so much power in their lives as he closed the door shut. He shook his head disapprovingly as he turned the key in the ignition. He smiled when he clicked his seatbelt and looked at the house he built with this truck.

My granddad loved this truck because of what it afforded him. He provided for his family, and the truck was a means of keeping them happy. He would give his life for his children, but he didn't want to choose between the truck and his son. He felt that should have never been a thing. Why couldn't my dad just see that he was giving us everything he had?

His prayer must have reached my dad's heart because he was led to call him that day. But he had to run to the bathroom first, and my grandfather beat him to the punch. As Granddad drove out of the driveway and entered the open road, he was ready to talk after cooling off, and of course, my dad missed the call because he was in the bathroom.

"Hey, Son, I tried to catch you. Hey, look, I am sorry to have put so much pressure on you lately. You are right; our problem shouldn't be the problems of the business. I love you, Son. I will call you back after a while."

He felt warmth in his heart when he hung up, but there was an icy breeze blowing in the window, cutting through his coat, hitting his body, and sending a chill through his bones. He grew very cold instantly, and his body felt a bit hard to move. It was like he was lethargic, and his energy was instantly tapped. The lights that he saw beaming in his direction all these years, on tonight, felt like lasers. He thought of pulling over when his vision was temporarily blurred.

If he had more strength in his body, he would have been alarmed. He was stuck with his hands on the wheel, and although he wanted to stop, he couldn't. Fear fell into his heart, and his eyes could read the internal message. He was having a stroke.

He saw the light blink on from the phone, and it read Gerald. He tried to move his hands, but with all his strength, he only managed to move his eyes and his head far enough to look at his phone. He tried to move his hands, but they only shook the steering wheel.

He was growing angry and frustrated with his own body; it had forsaken him. Yet he could not give up on trying to answer the phone. He grew tunnel vision and lost sight of the cars around him. His eyes locked onto the phone, and he tried again to move his hands, but the steering wheel kept him locked in place.

As he sped down the highway, with his foot locked onto the gas pedal, which couldn't switch to brake, he kept traveling down the highway. He looked up, remembering how quickly he was driving, but not sure of where to go. As he looked up, he noticed he wasn't on the highway anymore. He was driving across the grass, and he tried with his might to put his foot on the brakes, but his feet were not working. He saw nothing in front of him; trees were far off.

He hit a bump that landed him on his phone, and he heard Gerald say, "Hello, Dad?" Only garbled noises were heard from the other end of the phone, and then a huge crash occurred, and the phone went dead. My dad was unsure of what he had just heard, so he called back. The phone went straight to voicemail, and he decided to track Granddad's phone to see where he was.

My dad told Grandma he would be back and had to go and check on his dad. On the drive, my dad's stomach was in knots. He didn't know why today the noise around him couldn't be heard. He hadn't been behind the wheel since his accident and wasn't sure if that was a good idea. He knew that if something was wrong, Grandma would be the last person he wanted to find out.

She has been having crying spells ever since Granddad and my dad started fighting. It was the hardest on her, and my dad hated that. He hated being the source of her pain and the thorn in Granddad's side.

My dad had great parents to whom he was grateful, although his late actions made him look selfish. He never meant to hurt anyone; he just needed a bit of help, and perhaps he had gone about it wrong. He had a million thoughts as he drove down the street.

My granddad was about two hours away from the house. My dad was relieved when he was about ten minutes away. As he came up the hill, a short transition turned into miles of traffic. There were people standing outside their cars. He checked the app to see if there was a crash, and it was.

He prayed for it to be moved quickly so he could get past the accident and find his father. Traffic started to crawl forward, and he guessed people either stopped being so nosy or the emergency personnel got any debris out of their way. As my dad kept creeping up the highway, he saw tracks that ran across several lanes.

Dad slowed down with traffic to look around and see what he could see. He saw more tire-paved tracks that led off the highway. He said, "These kids could get somebody killed doing this stuff. The worst drivers were born during Covid." He shook his head in disappointment as he nearly cleared the traffic. He saw the back of a truck and discovered it wasn't silly kids playing with cars, but a semi ran off the highway and into the wall, protecting houses from the highway.

"Man, thank God that wall was there, or that truck would have gone–" My dad's eyes darted forward as he recognized the plate on the truck. "No, no, no, this can't be dad. God, tell me this isn't Dad!" He pulled over behind the cars in the right lane and attempted to get over into the grass. The officers outside and the fire department were trying to shoo traffic along. My dad didn't park the car and barely got it into park before jumping out.

"Hey, that is my dad. Is he alright? What happened?"

"Sir, we need you to get back in your vehicle."

"No, I can't get into my vehicle until you tell me if my dad is alright."

"Look, we can't say anything for certain yet. The paramedics are here and doing everything they can."

"Don't tell me that. Please don't tell me that."

"Sir, I am going to have to ask you to get back into your vehicle and stay there. I will come back to you, I promise. Just give us a minute."

Two other officers walked over to my dad because he looked as if he wanted to bolt to the semi, even though his legs would give out before he could get there. The stretcher was pushed into the back of the van as my dad watched his father with an oxygen mask on his face. Grandpa wasn't moving, but that didn't mean anything.

My dad couldn't hear himself or see how he was acting, but he was breathing quickly. He was in pain because he fell, and his arm was out of the sling, and his knees bent from hitting the ground. He was screaming in physical pain, and his soul was responding. The paramedics came over and asked the cops what was happening, "I think he might be the guy's son."

My dad was passing out; he closed his eyes, and blackness replaced the scene of the accident. His hurting body was walked to the paramedic van. They tried to keep him lifted up because when he bent down, he cried out louder. He groaned from the sharp pain felt in his ribs. They asked him, "Sir, what is hurting?"

"My, my ribs, oh God." They checked under his shirt, and he was bleeding. They had him lay down on the small bench in the back of the para-medic, and they tended to his injury. The paramedic driver was doing ninety down the highway to get my grandfather and dad to the hospital. If my dad could think, the only thing he didn't want to think about was his mother getting this call.

How sad would it be to hear both her son and husband are being rushed to the hospital in the same paramedic vehicle? It didn't sound good, but that was the case. They both were rushed to the ER.

Luckily, my dad went to the same hospital as before, and so they called Grandma back to the hospital. After hanging up the phone, Grandma had no one else to call but my mom. The phone rang and rang. Grandma called back, "Please pick up. Please pick up." She prayed and cried while she waited for my mom to answer her phone.

The phone went to voicemail again, and Grandma cried out, "God, please, please don't let this happen to me. Please don't let something hap-pen to my husband and my son and I am not there. God–" The phone rang, and she quickly answered.

"Hello, Kristina?"

"Yea? Did you mean to call me?"

"Yes, I need to go to the hospital to check on my husband and son. Can I bring Kimberly by you?"

"I mean, yeah, of course. Are they alright?"

"I don't know. They are both in the ER."

"Oh God. Yes, I will text you my address."
The ladies hang up, and Jasmine enters the room.

"Hey, I am about to head out. Are you ready?"

My mom was wearing a form-fitting red dress, had her hair done, and heels on. She didn't look up as she texted, "No, I'm not going. Something just happened, and Kimmie is on her way here."

"Why?"

"I am not sure, but Gerald is in the ER, and I think his father is too."

"Oh, dang. You need me to do something?"

"No, you go ahead. I am sure it will be a long night if that is cool."

"Yeah, that's fine. We know you don't like going over there."

"Girl, I have a creepy neighbor, and I swear I hate living in the hood."

"You shouldn't have moved out so quickly."

"The place looked good in the pictures."

"Rule number one, never rent a place without going by at night a few times, both during the week and the weekend. Not all these nice places have outstanding people living there. Some of them house the hood." She giggles and says, "But girl, I gotta go, bye. Call me if you need me." She hears a beep outside the door from her ride and gives my mom a quick hug before exiting. My mother goes to her friend's room and changes into some comfy pajamas.

About fifteen minutes later, there was a knock on the door. My mom opens the door to her ex-mother-in-law. "Hey, sorry to come around without much notice and barge in on your time."

"No, it is totally fine. Hey Kimmie." I walked forward and hugged her per usual. "We are going to be good. Do whatever you need to, and tell Gerald and his father. I pray they get well soon."

"Thank you, Kristina, I appreciate that." Grandma leaves the door, and my mom asks, "Hey, Kimmie, are you hungry?"

"A little; we had dinner already."

"Well, that means we can skip to dessert. Want some ice cream?"

"Yes, please!" The two of us went to the kitchen to find ice cream and the fixings. We grabbed bowls big spoons, and create our own ice cream sundaes. We had sprinkles and caramel drizzle on top for that extra boost. The only thing missing was the cherry on top; I guess you can't have it all all the time.

Mom and I went in front of the tv to watch cartoons until we both fell asleep. It was one of my fondest memories with my mother. She honestly started to try to get along with me when I could go to school. I guess the baby phase was the part she was the most nervous about. It was nice to be around her when it was just her and I.

Being close to my mom on that day made me want to live with her again. I never told my dad that because there seemed to never be a good time. I saw how hard he worked, but I also saw how hard my mom worked, too — to get her life back on track after "the creep"–her words, not mine.

Although I don't clearly remember him, (Javier) Mom made sure he never knew where we moved to. I only knew his name in case she saw him on the street. My mom insisted on having secret words to announce distress, and Javier's name was a trigger for her. She was a good mother who I knew wanted to keep me safe.

It was weird how she apologized randomly to me for how things were. I don't remember the police-supervised visits. I don't think those were ever necessary. It was hard growing up with my dad and not seeing her as much. I wanted more time with my mom.

I loved my dad, but he didn't understand me as well as I would have liked. He just grew busy with the details of caring for me, so playdates slowed down. He didn't get fashion and doing my hair, and my grandmother's style was very much set in the 60s. I was stuck in a time warp, but with my mom, she knew what to do to bring me to the current day.

Mom was fun and always wanted to do something cool. She wore sexy clothes, and I would dress up in her clothes while she was sleeping. I even put on her heels to see if I could do it, and honestly, I felt my ankle give way, and my foot slid sideways. Both my knees hit the floor as I fell. That was the last time I wore them shoes, too.

Waiting around for my grandmother to

come back took two days. She wasn't smiling, and my dad wasn't either. I asked them what was wrong, but no one wanted to tell me. The house was so quiet, and I desperately wanted to leave. Grandma stopped cooking, and Dad would just order out.

We had some people from the neighborhood bring us dishes sometimes, and I ate them. It was so good to have plates of food that weren't french fries and chicken nuggets. At first, I loved it because my grandma never let me have it. She always said fried food is not good for you all the time. But my dad would sneak out to get it whenever he could.

Ordering online because he was bedridden again was all he could do. My grandma seemed to stay in the bed all day. I came to her room and asked to play, but she would barely speak. I asked Dad, "Dad, is grandma mad at me?"

"No, baby, why would you think that?"

"She doesn't play with me no more."

"Oh, no, baby girl. It is not you. Grandma is just a little sad right now."

"Is it because Granddaddy is sick?"

"Yes."

"Oh, okay. When is he coming home?"

"The doctors said they are not sure. They are still monitoring him."

"Okay, can I go and see him?"

"No, they don't allow little children where he is."

"Dad, I am not a baby."

"I know, but only adults can go."

"Oh, okay. I pray I can see him soon. I really want Grandma to feel better." My dad gives me a hug and replies, "Yeah, me too."

That was the longest week for my grandmother. She didn't speak at all, and I can only remember seeing her come to the table twice to eat. I wasn't sure what really happened, but I had a bad feeling Grandpa wasn't coming back, and they didn't want to tell me.

The phone rang one day, and I heard my grandma call for my dad. They put the phone on speaker and turned the phone's volume down. I knew when they told me not to come into the room, it was bad news. It wasn't, but a few moments later, I heard my grandmother start screaming. I thought to run into the room, but my feet stayed glued to the floor.

What was I going to do? What could I say to make things better? I was only a kid, and now, I was a kid without a grandfather.

I never had a grandfather on my mother's side. Her mom died–or at least that was what I was told, and her grandmother raised her. Her grandmother, I didn't see too much lately. She was moved to a nursing home, and her house was sold. It seems like each time we go to visit her, she cries about losing her house; she really loved it.

I felt helpless in stopping her from crying. No matter how many hugs I gave, she wouldn't stop. They did seem to make her feel better, though. So, I kept giving them. I knocked on the door, and I heard my dad's feet shuffle the fastest they had in days to the door. "Hey, Kimmie, grandma is okay. Just give us a minute, and I will be out, okay?"

I nodded my head, yes, but I guessed what had happened. I sat on the couch and cried as I listened to my grandmother crying in the other room. I didn't really know what had happened at that moment; it would be many years later that I learned the truth. My grandad had a stroke and crashed into a wall.

The stroke put him into a comma. He had broken bones and internal bleeding, but his body was fighting to live, although his brain was shutting down. He had a war happening within his body, and without life support, his lungs would have collapsed, his heart would stop beating, and his brain would drift into an eternal rest.

We could have never thought of how tired Grandpa's body was. The next few weeks were brutal for my grandmother. The strongest support for my father he now had to support. The plans for our house ended that day, and my family life structure changed permanently.

First, my dad had to go and give the official approval to pull the plug. I wasn't allowed in the room before, so my last goodbye to my grandpa would be at his funeral. I remember walking up to the casket, thinking to see him and tell him what I couldn't before. However, when I looked into the casket, I didn't see a man that looked like my granddad. His face looked droopy. His eyes were closed, he had no smile, and I cried because I wondered if he died happy or sad.

I wanted my grandpa to pick me up and play airplane just one last time because my dad stopped doing that after the accident. My grandpa was telling jokes when he was at home, and he made time for me. He would give me candy and always say, I can have an extra scoop of ice cream. I missed him saying that at dinner.

I wanted my dad and granddad to stop fighting, but I never thought the fighting would end because he died. I went back to my chair, and I didn't hold his hand because I was scared. I wasn't sure what to do, and I couldn't ask my grandmother or dad. They were both crying too badly. I knew, based on their reactions, that my grandpa was truly gone. But now, how can I say goodbye if I have to sit down?

As a child, the service felt long. I don't remember how long it was, but I know I fell asleep for a little bit of it. My dad nudged me to wake up so our family could walk back to the coffin. This was it. I had one last time to say goodbye to my grandpa.

I looked in the coffin, and I said, "Granddaddy, I pray you are happy. I know you look sad right now, but I pray you are happy in heaven. Love you, and I miss you." Tears rolled from my eyes, and my words seemed to be a gentle knife piercing into my grandma's heart. She sat back down three times before she came up for the last pass.

Her legs seemed to give out from underneath her, and my dad supported her back to her seat, where she cried even more. There were men who came who picked up different corners of the casket, and they walked my grandpa out of the church and put him into this long van. They drove away with his body, and we followed behind in our cars.

We drove several blocks to the cemetery, where he was put deep into the ground. They said another prayer there, and we all threw roses onto the casket before they added the dirt. I thought we were staying until they were done putting all the dirt back, but my dad said we could leave.

It was a quiet ride back home, and it was quiet for many months after that. Then, the calls started coming in. The time it took to plan the funeral and begin to grieve the death of my grandfather, I guess no one made time to check the mail. My granddad's accident tore up a big wall, and his insurance didn't cover all the damages. My granddad's company was being sued by the state for the balance.

Although my dad worked very hard to save the company, it didn't prevent him from losing it. My grandma put up the house for sale to help buy us time and allow us to have a life because, without my grandfather's income, we had to live off our savings.

With my dad still struggling to recuperate and finding out he might have a punctured lung, we were scared to have him do more to save the company. The doctors said because of his healing journey, he was at risk for re-expansion, heart failure, or respiratory failure. He was a risk behind the wheel, and my grandma couldn't chance anything happening to him.

She rushed to put him on disability, which meant he could no longer drive. Our family, which was so stable, became very unstable in a matter of months. My grandpa wasn't lying when he said the company couldn't afford medical bills. We were living off his savings for years and didn't know it.

With shooting gas prices, mileage changes, and picking up loads that weren't there. And with all the chaos that comes with running a trucking business, Granddad was losing money at every turn. The big companies were gobbling up smaller contracts to survive, and that meant he had to take anything–even jobs that put him practically at a loss.

My granddad used all he had to try and leave something for my dad and me. But the City took everything we could have had, and if it wasn't for my grandma selling her house, which she had before marrying my grandfather, we wouldn't have had a dime.

We became poor, homeless, and had very little to live off of. After five years, I was sent to live with my mother because my grandma and father were both sent to live in respective homes made to deal with their conditions. It was like after my grandpa died, they both gave up. My grandma gave in to loneliness, and when my dad lost the business, it was as if my dad died with it, too.

Dad never forgave himself for fighting with his dad about money. My mom tried to help me understand it all. She would tell me, "Money isn't everything, but it buys stability. Never be without money because it can make a bad situation unbearable. But if you don't have it, choose to live anyway. Money doesn't buy happiness."

I didn't see how money could have changed the outcome of my grandfather dying, but she saw a connection. She was living very well. She had her own house, although she never told my dad. She also made me promise not to tell. She said, "Your dad will ask for more money if you tell him. And I don't think this is any of his business. This is a secret between you and me. Got it?"

I agreed to keep the secret, but I don't think my dad cared anyway. We were getting a house. He always told me, "We just had to give it a little more time." But that day never came. I cried the first night I was at my mom's because I wanted my dad to be there, too. I wanted to see him in his house, too, not in a little room on a bed.

My mom said she hated seeing him like that, so we came less and less to see him. I missed him, but telling her I wanted to go see him seemed to make her upset, so I started to ask less. I thought, where would I go if my mom got rid of me? I had no father, grandmother, or anybody. I saw how my mom treated her mother, and she barely saw her either. Why would I be any different?

I was on guard, and I tried not to make her angry. Normally, she was calm and only yelled sometimes. But whenever I asked for help with my homework or to go places when she got off work–that wasn't the mall and needed money, she seemed to yell a lot more.

Even though my mom paid child support, she didn't pay nowhere near what my dad was paying over the years to take care of me. She was paying only $100 a week or something because she was unemployed when the order was issued. My dad never went back to court. He always said, "You are my child. Your mom don't have to do nothing. She can keep her money. I will take care of you myself." So, I guess it was her turn to take care of me herself, too.

Mom was not as nice as dad about it. I wouldn't say I hated living at my mom's house, but it was a challenge. I thought she was going to have more movie nights with me, but she didn't. I thought we would get our hair and nails done and do stuff together, but we didn't. She bought food on the app like my father did, and she would leave me with Jasmine so she could to have "adult time." Living with her was not like living with my dad and grandparents.

I cried a lot, I mean a lot. I cried at home in my bed. I cried at school. I couldn't stop crying. I guess I was hurting. I remember one day, my teacher called my name, and I just kept lying on the desk. She called me, and I heard her, "Kimberly! Kimberly, I need you to pick your head up right now." I didn't move.

She got up from her desk and said, "That's it. I am calling the principal, and we are calling your mother, too." The class, in a choir voice, said, "Oohh." I was getting embarrassed while tears ran hot down my face. I couldn't get up. I had water all over my desk, and I knew people would call me "Crybaby," but I stopped caring. The insult lost its sting a long time ago.

My teacher took me by my arm firmly but gently and walked me to the door of the classroom. She signaled across the classroom to have another teacher to watch over her class. She told the other students to keep working until she got back. We walked briskly down the hallway to the principal's office. I had not been to his office yet.

She spoke to the ladies at the administration desk when we arrived, and they told me to take a seat. She came up to me and said, "Kimberly, you really need to speak to someone about how you feel. I understand if it is not me, but honey, it is not fair to you to put yourself through all this pain. Do you understand what I am saying?"

I nodded but didn't say a word. I cried a bit more, sitting there looking out the window. The principal was walking the halls and blowing his whistle, so I knew it could be a minute before he emerged. I was almost asleep in the chair until I heard, "prrrrt." The whistle quickened my spirit back to my body, and I popped up.

"Young lady, meet me in my office, please," said the principal. He was followed by the school's guidance counselor, Mrs. Jace. "Tell me, how are you doing?" Although his whistle was loud and obnoxious, he had a sweet spirit that we all liked. I wanted to answer him, but nothing came out. Mrs. Jace took the next swing, "Kimberly, I understand that you lost your grandfather recently. Is that right?"

I nodded my head yes. "Are you sad about that?"

Once more, I nodded my head yes. Mrs. Jance asks, "Is that why you are crying?" I shook my head no.

"So why are you crying, honey? Is everything alright at home?"

I didn't say anything but looked to the floor. "Kimberly, can you look at me, please?" I looked up to Mrs. Jace. "Is everything alright at home?" I could not help it and started crying again. The counselor takes a moment and takes the principal aside. The two of them have a conversation.

The principal leaves the room, and Mrs. Jace comes back to me. "Kimberly, if there is something wrong happening at home, you know you can tell me, right?"

I shake my head no. Mrs. Jace responds, "Yes, you can. You can tell me anything. We are here to help you. You know that, right?"

I wipe my tears with the tissue Mrs. Jace gave me. I started to speak, "I am not happy."

"Why are you not happy?"

"Because, because…"

"You can say it, what's wrong?"

"I don't feel like my mom loves me."

"Why would you say that?"

"Because she doesn't play with me. We don't cook together or eat ice cream anymore. She yells a lot at me."

"She does?"

"Yea. It makes me sad."

"I can see how that can make you sad. I would be sad, too." The principal comes back into the room with a lady dressed in business pants and a suit jacket. She seems nice as she introduces herself.

I felt like a pin was stuck in a pressure-filled boil. When my feelings came out like warm liquid as I talked to the lady, I was feeling much calmer. I wouldn't say that I was happy, but I was less sad. She said she would reach out to my mother so we can all work together. I was excited about that. I just knew things would get better after this meeting.

My mom came to the school and picked me up early. The lady couldn't wait around for her to come on that day but said she would come by the house at her next available time to see how things were going. I looked forward to seeing her again.

She came into the office looking happy to see me when she picked me up. She was smiling and happy-go-lucky with the woman at the front desk. She was honestly a bit happier than she is normally. I guess that is what parents do when they have to come to school in the middle of the work-day.

She grabbed me by my hand, and together, we walked out of the building. I was surprised by the gesture because we don't normally hold hands, especially now. My dad was big on holding hands, but now, not so much. We get inside the car, and before we can get out of the parking lot, she turns to me and starts in.

"What the hell is wrong with you?" Stunned, I looked to the floor.

"Look at me when I am talking to you." I looked up from the floor and to my mother. "Do you know the stuff you told that lady got her thinking I am a neglectful mother?"

I shook my head no because I wasn't sure what she was saying.

She said, "That lady is not here to help you. She comes to take people's children away. Do you want to live somewhere else?"

I shook my head no.

"Then you better learn how to keep your mouth shut about my business. Don't you eat every day?"

I shook my head yes.

"You have clothes and a house to live in, running water, and you don't want for nothing. So why are you telling this lady there are problems at home?"

I was silent. I knew no matter what I had to say, it would be the wrong answer.

"Don't you hear me talking to you? Say something. I know you hear me!"

"No, Mom. I was just telling the lady that I was sad because–"

"You are sad. How do you sound right now? I am home all day, and I ask you questions. You never once told me there was a problem."

I couldn't finish my sentence, and I knew she wouldn't hear me. I felt in my bones that I was misunderstood by my mother. It sucks that I am still alone, and now things are worse since that nice lady, who I guess wasn't so nice either.

As an attempt to defuse her anger, I reply, "Sorry, Mom. It won't happen again."

"I best know dang well it won't. Girl, you got me embarrassed to come up to this school. They look at me like I am a poor, impoverished, and ghetto momma. I hate that sh–stuff. If you have a problem, you talk to me, not the lady at your school. Got it?"

I knew a trap when I saw one a mile away. This was a trap. Whenever a black momma says, "Say that again," "You can tell me anything," or "Do it again, come on." It is best to avoid doing or saying anything. You just learn to suck it up!

I learned subconsciously I could not rely on my mother as a person who could talk to me. She would yell at the slightest things, which I hate. My father and grandparents were nothing like my mother. I guess I would have to learn how to deal with her.

The rest of the ride was silent. I was relieved when we parked, and I could escape her glaring at me. She told me, "Oh, by the way, you are grounded. No technology until Friday since you want to run your mouth. And because you don't like the food that I buy, you can go to the kitchen and make yourself a sandwich and have some chips tonight. I am ordering steak and potatoes."

My mom heads to her room and closes the door. Often, she is in there anyhow, so nothing was new. It would be so boring being in this house with no technology. The only thing I could think of was to read books. I have already read my books, so not sure what else to do. After eating my sandwich, I got in my bed and went to sleep.

For a year, my mom and I tiptoed around each other. I was sure not to bother her and said as little as possible. She stayed on the computer, so she wasn't attentive to anything that didn't deal with medical coding. My mom made great money, and working two jobs meant she earned at least a hundred thousand a year.

She didn't talk much about it to everyone else, but she made certain to point it out with the items she bought and how often we went shopping. My mom didn't deny me clothes, shoes, or anything that made me look great. I had the latest fashion and the most updated phone. She cared about stuff like that.

I was grateful, but I cannot say that it meant that much to me. Some of the other kids would say, "That's because you got it. If you didn't, you would know how the rest of us feel."

"I am grateful for my mom," I would say. And they would reply, "No, you're not. You are spoiled." For some reason, hearing that made my skin crawl. I wasn't spoiled, and I couldn't say anything about why my picture-perfect life was a nightmare. I had no one to talk to. My mom had no friends with children. I was an only child. So, all the attention was on me.

Until one day, I found out she had a boy-friend. My mom and her relationships were always a mystery to me. I would hear noises late into the evening, but I knew better than to ask. She had her fun at night. I assumed she didn't want me to know, and that was why she had never spoken about it.

But this guy and her, if he is the same one from when the noises started, have been going out for about eight months now. When I came home from school, I saw him sitting at the table. He was dressed in business clothes and wore glasses. Unimpressed, I said to my mom, "Hey. How is work going?"

"Good, Kimmie. Hey. I want you to meet someone." She points to the man sitting at the table, who looks a bit nervous. He stands up from the table and reaches out his hand in an attempt to shake mine." I gave a half smile and waved once. "Nice to meet you."

"Oh, my name is Greg."

"Okay, hey Greg." I look toward my mom, and she gives me a stiff nod, and I say, "Nice to meet you."

"I've been wanting to meet you for some time now. I hear you go to the elementary school my daughter goes to."

"Who's your daughter?"

"Ariana."

"I don't think I know her."

"Yeah, you have different teachers, I think. When you head to middle school, I am sure you will have her in your classes if you stay in the district."

My mom replies, "Yeah, I don't see us moving. I bought this house, and I ain't going nowhere."

"So, I guess I will see her around." I took a juice from the fridge. "Mom, I gotta go do my homework." She nodded okay, and I left the kitchen.

I don't know why I didn't get a warm feeling about this guy. I'm not sure if it is because I don't think any man will be as good as my dad or that I didn't need a stepdad.

He tried to build a relationship over the next few months, but I admit that I was closed off. I didn't want to like him–but I wasn't rude. I just wanted to be clear that I had a father, and things for me were good–even if they weren't.

We had a talk one day when he brought his daughter over for a cookout. "Hey, you know you don't have to think I want to take your father's place."

"Yeah, I know."

"It's okay to get to know me, too. I am not a bad guy."

"Uhuhn." At the right time, his daughter walked up and said, "Hey, nice house." I replied, relieved, "Thanks." Greg jumps in, "I will let you two girls talk. But think about what I said, Kimberly; will you?"

Ariana took me by my hand and walked with me in the other direction. "Hey, I just saved you."

"Tell me about it."

"So, you ready to go to middle school?"

"I don't know, I guess."

"It's going to be so much fun. There are parties, new friends, older boys, and new ones. I hear the boys in middle school have muscles."

"Girl, is that all you gonna talk about?"

170

"No, I am just joking, but not about the boy part." She starts laughing. "But seriously. No, my dad can be a pain when he wants to get his point across. He is a good guy but can be annoying."

"I think that is all parents."

"Your mom sounds cool."

"Yeah, she is alright."

"Do you think they are going to get married?"

"I don't know. I guess that that is between them."

"Yeah, of course, but you can have an opinion."

"Hmmm. Having you as a sister doesn't sound bad," I replied. She grabs me and says, "You better have said that." We joked and horse-around while enjoying the party.

Middle School

We girls grew close over the summer, and it was as if the two of us had moved in. Middle school was nothing like elementary school for me. It was bigger kids, louder noises, and some mean teachers. To be fair, there were some girls who talked back to teachers like they were grown. I felt bad for some of the teachers.

But I knew better than to jump into other people's mess. I stayed quiet and trusted the process. Somehow, Ariana rose to the top in school. Everybody loved her, and I did, too. She invited me to the parties she got invitations for, and I turned down most of them.

It wasn't until I met Raymond that I knew I had to hang out more with Ariana. The only problem was that I couldn't get out of the house like she did. Both of our parents were at my house, while Ariana only had her mother to deal with, who worked a lot. Although Ariana's dad tried to keep tabs on her, she would leave her phone at home and sneak out.

She told me I should try it, but I feared what my mom would do if she ever found out I did something like that. But this was going to be a party that I knew Raymond would be at. I wanted to know what happened at these parties anyway. Ariana told me the basics, like don't take a cup from anyone you don't know. Never be alone with a boy. And don't trust strangers, girls, and guys.

The checklist was very short, so I was confident to head to the party. I had party clothes, so that wasn't an issue either. What was the issue was getting past my mother. I waited until the music was up and blasting from my mom's tv. This was the norm, it seemed, and she couldn't fall asleep without noise. After letting the tv play for about thirty minutes, I left out the door. I knew that one house alarm sensor was broken.

We had an appointment for the security people to come out and fix it, but I knew that was a sign from God. If it wasn't for that thing hitting the floor a few times by yours truly, who was to say if I could have ever found a way out? I got to the backyard and headed for the gate. Only the thing was locked.

How could I have been so stupid and forgotten we had locked it with a keyed lock? I couldn't go back into the house; it felt like bad energy. I needed to jump the gate. The gate wasn't that tall, but I worried mostly about the noise. I wore the right shoes, sneakers, so getting over it wouldn't be incredibly difficult.

I started to step up on the first wooden beam, but there was too much space between the second wood piece. I looked for something to wedge my feet on to help me reach the higher wooden beam, and I found something. One of the patio chairs. I moved it as quietly as I could up against the fence's gate. I was able to easily reach the second beam, but I would have to tumble over the wall.

I went over the wall less than ideal and ended up landing on a hill that broke my fall but didn't stop my underwear from showing. I don't know why I wore a pleated skirt to escape the backyard. I wasn't sure if someone heard me because, hitting the ground, I did let out a groan. I rolled over and tried to get presentable as quickly as possible. Thank God for the backlight, yes, but the dark surrounding to shield my embarrassment.

I got up and started walking a little slow in the beginning until my legs were certain they were good. I definitely needed a better plan for getting back inside. I was able to get to the corner of the street and meet up with Ariana.

"You ready to go see Raymond?" I giggled, and we both walked down the street, talking about how great of a time we were going to have. Getting to the house from the outside looked quiet. We came to the side door and came in. We walked downstairs to the basement, and that is when the noise became full blast.

The lights were blue, and Ariana was quickly dragged away. "I will be back; go and have fun." She was off, and I had three rules to follow. I looked around the room to find a place to go and hide. I felt so out of place just standing there like a dud.

Then I felt someone grab my hand. "Hey." I pulled my hand back and turned around; it was Raymond. In my head, I thought, wow, oh my God, it is Raymond. I know my eyes looked off because looking at him in his eyes made me so nervous. I didn't respond initially, and I felt worse.

He didn't back off, though, and said, "Hey, I'm Raymond. Welcome to my party."

"You live here?"

"Yeah."

"It's a nice house. I didn't know you lived so close to me."

"So you know me?"

"Of course, I've seen you at school, and I know who you are."

"Good, so this doesn't have to be awkward. You want something to drink?"

"Yeah, sure."

"Okay, I will go get it for you."

"Actually, I can go with you." I walked with him, praying wherever the drinks were would not take me to a secluded place. It was actually more light where the drinks were, and it was canned soda. I thought the worst from watching movies. It was cool to see him in the light. He was more fine in the light than under the blue lights.

"So, how's school?"

"It's cool." I couldn't believe the person I came here for was talking to me! I liked him, and I thought he might have known, but I was too shy to ever introduce myself. I know I should be over this by now, but I am still nervous when talking to new people. It's been about four weeks since school started, and I haven't talked to everyone in my classes yet. I guess I am just a slow socialite.

Time passed, and I honestly forgot about Ariana. The party for me was winding down because I couldn't risk getting caught; it was getting late. I told Raymond that I had to go. He replied, "I could walk you home."

"Are you sure? This is your party. Why would you leave it?"

"Because I live here and can just come back home. Really, it's no big deal. "

I looked for Ariana one more time and found her. "Hey, you ready to go?"

"Not yet. I am going to stay a bit later."

"Okay, well, I am going to walk home."

"Do you want me to walk you?"

"No, Raymond said he would do it. He is waiting for me upstairs."

"Okay, look at you. Coming to the party and pulling the guy you want."

"It's not like that." We both start to laugh as I walk away. I was excited to have Ariana as a sister to me, who was so cool and my age, too. I may not be the biggest fan of her father, but I love her like a sister. I got upstairs, and Raymond was waiting for me.

We started walking to my house and talking more about random stuff. He could have been talking about crickets, and I would have been interested. I just found myself looking at him more than I cared to admit. I was so focused on him that I didn't see the stop sign I walked straight into.

"Hey, dang, you good?"

More embarrassed than in pain, I replied, "Yeah, all good." We both laughed about it, and he cracked a few jokes to lighten the mood. He knew what to do to keep the conversation going. We arrived at my house, and he came up to me and hugged me. His arms felt so warm, and I gave him a quick kiss on the cheek.

He smiled and, with a grin, said, "Alright, Kimberly, I will see you tomorrow at school." "You can call me Kimmie." He nodded and turned back toward his house. I headed for the gate and felt light enough to fly! I was on cloud nine, and I almost forgot I needed to climb the gate to get back in. There are no wooden beams on the front side, so how was I going to get up?

I looked and saw the garbage can and knew the best way over was to stand on top of it. I am praying this thing doesn't cave in because I don't know if there is trash in it or not. I moved it to the fence and hopped over it uneventfully. I was able to step into the chair on the other side. I got down and moved it back, making as little noise as I could.

I went to the sliding glass door and looked in to see if anyone was there. I didn't see lights on, so I assumed the area was clear. I opened the door, closed it behind me, and locked it. As soon as I did that, the light flicked on. My heart jumped through my body and touched the sky.

I turned to see who was turning the switch, and it was Greg. "Now, where have you been?"

"Ugh."

"Let me guess, at a party? You are a good girl; why are you sneaking out of the house?"

"I just–"

"Wanted to hang out with your friends?"

I nodded my head yes and shrugged my shoulders. He took an audible breath and replied, "You know guys only want one thing from you at this age. They can't marry you or take care of you, and many of them want to see how far you will let them go."

"Yeah, I know. It was nothing like that."

"So that kiss you did was nothing?"

"Are you spying on me?"

"No, you were in the front yard. I am going to have to tell your mom about this."

"Come on, Greg. Why would you do that?

Can't this be a secret?"

"You want me to keep something from your mom?"

"I mean, does she really need to know?"

"So you don't think she needs to know you kissed a boy?"

"It wasn't like that. It was only on the cheek."

"So if I told you I would keep a secret if you kissed me on the cheek, what would you do?" Without hesitation, I came up to Greg and gave him a kiss on the cheek. Then I said, "See, it's not a big deal."

"Now, I am calling your mother for real."

"What?"

"If you would do this, ain't no telling what you would do if something asked you to Kimberly. Your mom needs to know." He took off out of the kitchen, and I followed behind him. He went into the room, and I knew it was too late to say a word. "Babe, I need you to get up," he says to my mom.

My mom slowly woke up, "What?"

"I need you to get up for a second."

My mom sits up in her bed, "Yes, what?"

"I just caught your daughter creeping back into the house."

"Wait, what are you talking about?"

"Your little Kimmie just got busted crawling

over the gate and coming in through the backyard."

"Really?" My mom sits up.

"Yes, and she kissed a boy in the front yard. But that is not all. She asked me to keep a secret, and I told her I was waking you up right now to tell you."

"Okay,"

"And then, to test her, I said if she wanted me to keep a secret, kiss me on the cheek. She did, and that is what concerns me. She cannot think it is okay to be kissing boys and grown men to hold secrets. Imagine if I was that dude?"

"She did that?"

"Go ask her." My mom gets up from her bed and I listened for her footsteps bumping down the hall. She busts in the door and says, "Kimmie, what are you doing?"

"Look, Mom, I was just trying to–" Before I could get out another word, I felt fire sting my lips. I didn't see it coming. I should have turned on the lights. "You are not grown. You don't pay any bills, and you have no business creeping out of your room. And you kissed a boy?"

"It was only on the cheek!"

"Is that supposed to matter, Kimmie?"

I learned from the first slap to keep my mouth shut. She is pissed, and nothing I can say will calm her down. She goes on moving her arms, yelling, "Greg said you kissed him on the cheek to keep it a secret, Kimmie."

"Mom, it wasn't like that."

"So you comfortable kissing grown men, Kimmie? I told you about this. You never ever should have agreed to do that, ever! You know better."

"But Mom, it wasn't–" I felt the sting again. She slapped the words out of my mouth and got real close to my face. "You are not grown, Kimmie. Greg is not your man. The boy you kissed today is not your man. If I ever hear about you kissing anyone before you are grown and out of my mouth house, we are going to have a conversation, and it will be worse than this."

She backs up out of my face, and the fear that pushed my heart to the moon is still shooting up. I was scared and didn't realize I started backing up when she came close to my face. Her rage could be felt like steam coming from a pot, although you couldn't see it. I knew then I couldn't trust Greg, and I wanted nothing to do with him.

"You out here trying to be grown. You need to stay in a child's place. I am not raising no babies. So don't be out here doing anything that would make them." She slammed my door and stomped back to her room. I knew my mom was crazy before, but this is a whole nother level. If only Greg knew his daughter was out tonight, too, and he is not the perfect parent, he thinks.

I got up and would have changed my clothes, but I was scared and glued to my mattress. I wasn't setting foot on the floor. I got under the covers and kept my eyes open because I wasn't sure what might come next. I don't know when I went to sleep, but I woke up to my alarm and Greg knocking at the door.

"Hey, get up. You are going to be late." His footsteps walked away, and I was glad. The last thing

I want is to see his face this morning. The stupid snitch couldn't be cool this one time. I hated him. I might be wrong to do so, but I don't care. He didn't have to do that.

I went to my closet and picked out my clothes. I was still a bit sleepy, and while walking to the bathroom, I was sure I looked like a zombie fighting the light. I put my clothes on the closed toilet seat and looked into the mirror. My eyes jumped wide when I saw my lip!

It was swollen and had a slight crack. "Oh my god." I couldn't raise my voice, and all I could do was cry. I was so embarrassed. I just had the time of my life with Raymond, and now I got to go to school looking like I had an allergic reaction to a bee sting! Why was life turning on me like this?

I heard Greg outside the door, "You are missing your bus. I told your mom I would take you."

The absolute last person I want to see. This day is just getting worse. I quickly put my clothes on and was careful when I washed my face and brushed my teeth. This lip stings. I came out of the bathroom, and Greg saw my face and said, "Wow, did you get stung by a bee or something?"

I lied and said, "Yeah. A bee." I walked past him and grabbed my backpack. I sat inside the car and didn't say anything but looked out the window. As he drove, he glanced back at me and put his hand on my thigh. "You know I had to tell your mom, right?"

I didn't look at him. I just kept looking out the window. "I was concerned about you, Kimmie. You are a pretty girl, and a lot of boys are going to try to get with you. I want to protect you from all of that. You believe me, don't you?"

I smirked and turned my head to look out the window. "You can ignore me now, but you won't always feel this way." He just didn't know I would feel this way for a long time. I hated his guts. He is ruining my life, and he thinks I want to thank him for it? What an idiot. I couldn't wait for him to get his hand off my thigh and get away from me.

Going to school is getting me tons of attention, but not in the right way. Raymon spotted me, and he came up to me, "Hey, you good? What happened?"

"Yeah, I got stung by a bee last night."

"Dang girl, that looks bad."

"Yeah, allergies."

"You want to sit by me at lunch?"

"Yeah, of course." He gave me a quick hug and walked off. Ariana saw me and came up. "Hey, so how are things with Raymond–girl, what happened to your lip?" She didn't see the swollen side until mid-sentence.

"Yeah, got stung by a bee."

"Really? It did that?"

"Allergies"

"Maybe you should put something on it? It looks painful."

"Because it is. Can we talk about something else, please."

"Yeah, so how did things go last night with Raymond?"

"So good. We talked, and as you already know, he walked me home."

"That sounds good."

"Yeah, we will sit together at lunch."

"Okay, well, I will see you at lunch." Ariana had to take off to her class. We don't share the first period together. I felt crummy going into the class and seeing everyone looking and talking. I felt like every whisper was about me, although I am sure it wasn't. This day couldn't go by fast enough, and however long it would take for this lip to heal wouldn't be soon enough.

Sitting with Raymond at lunch did make the lip worth it. He was so kind and caring. He talked about sports today, and I just listened, perhaps like a mystified puppy with big eyes. I can't say I was in love because I don't know what that is, but I really liked him.

Coming home that day, I got the silent treatment, and that was no surprise. My mom thinks I am fast because of a side kiss. I was not grown, yes, but I am also not a baby. I am growing up, and I don't understand why she is making such a big deal.

Greg tried several times that week to get my attention. He would touch my shoulder, sit next to me on the couch, and offer to take me places. None of that was convincing me he was authentic or gave a dang about my life. He was a snitch. Now, I see why they say snitches get stitches.

My mom had to go into the office for a week of training, and Greg was in charge. I think he was too excited to try and tell me what to do. Every time he came around, I went somewhere else, but this week, he was unavoidable. I was doing my homework in my room at my desk, and he came in and popped my headphones off to ask if I was hungry.

I didn't like him being in my room, so I came to the kitchen. I remember Ariana's rules: trust no one and never be alone with a guy. I wasn't sure if it went for stepfathers, too, but in case. Right now, I feel like my mother likes this guy more than me. I don't know why she likes him.

He is not ugly if I am honest, but I feel that he is a bit sneaky. Why would he set me up like that if he was going to tell her anyway? That was just the ultimate betrayal. He made us lunch and sat it at the table. I nodded to give my thanks.

He lifted my headphones again and said, "Aren't you going to say thank you?"

"I did, but thanks," I replied as I slid the headphones back onto my ears. I didn't start eating right away, and with him hovering over me, I didn't have an appetite at all. But the eerie feeling wouldn't shake until he moved, so I stopped writing and started eating. He replied, "Thank you. School is important, but you still have to eat." He put his hands on both of my shoulders, and he kissed me on the cheek.

"Hey, can you not do that?"

"What? Kiss you on the cheek?"

"Yeah, it makes me uncomfortable."

"But I thought kisses on the cheek didn't bother you?" He backs up and stands back.

"That was then. I don't know if you notice this or not. But I don't like you."

"Well, like I told you. I think you are going to grow to like me."

"Why would I do that? You snitched on me."

"You still mad about that?"

I said nothing but gave him the dumb stare because he deserved it.

"Girl, I cannot have your mom thinking I am a bad influence on you. It was an easy choice to rat you out." He comes back closer and grabs my boob. I swiped at him out of reflex.

"What are you doing?"

"Nothing."

"What do you mean you just grab–"

"Nothing. I am glad you wouldn't be stupid to let a boy do that."

"I am telling my mom."

"Yeah, and who do you think she is going to believe?"

"The girl sneaking around with boys?"

"She would believe me, Greg."

"If you tell her, I will just say you made it up."

She's my mom, and she will believe me." He leaves the kitchen with his phone. I am sure thinking of sending a text to my mom. I knew this guy was a creep, and now I know why. I couldn't wait for her to come through the door. He stayed in the room until she arrived.

The door opened, and I came up to her, "Mom, I need to talk to you."

"Yes, I need to talk to you too. What is this I am hearing about you cussing?"

"What?"

"Yeah, Greg told me you called him a bitch."

I was floored, and my jawline would need a crank to get it back closed. "I never said that. Mom, come on; why would I cuss?"

"So you calling Greg a liar?"

"Yes, mom. He is lying to you."

"Why would he lie on you, Kimmie?"

"Because he is a creep, and he grabbed me!"

"Come on, Kimmie. You get caught sneaking back into the house. He caught you kissing a boy, and then you kissed him on the cheek. I know I slapped you because you had to learn that behavior was not acceptable. But neither is this one: lying on people because you are mad or cussing them out. You are really surprising me."

"But mom–."

"Kimmie, let me tell you this one time. If you are making this up so you can get back at Greg, you need to stop it right now. If I hear anything else about you cussing, I am going to whoop you like you stole something. You are a lady, and ladies don't talk like that."

I knew better than to talk back, even though she was wrong. She doesn't believe me! This is crazy!

How am I uncomfortable in my home house while this creep gets to run free? "Well, Mom, can I be somewhere else until you get home?"

"You and Greg need to work this out. We are going to be a family, and sometimes parents have to do things children don't like. You need to respect him, Kimmie, and allow him to get to know you. I know it is hard with your dad not being around, but Greg is a good man, okay?"

I stared her blankly in the face. She looked off, and then she walked off. I heard the two of them talking when she got to her room, but he didn't come out for hours. I retreated to my room, and there was a knock on the door. "Yeah?"

Greg walks in, holding a plate of food. "Dinner for you." He set the plate on the table and tapped me on my hand before he left. If my eyes were lasers, I would have blown his head off. I was boiling, and I needed a plan.

I didn't get any good sleep that night because I was dreading the next day. I got up before my alarm, got dressed, and grabbed a light breakfast before darting out the door. I didn't want to see either one of them that morning. I went to school trying to focus and enjoy school life, but I was anxious about coming home.

I thought not to come home, but knew that would make things worse. I had to go home and face him. I entered the front door, and he was sitting on the couch. "Hey, how was school?"

I replied, "Fine," I tried to dart past him and to my room, but he cut me off. "How was your chat yesterday with Mom? Did it go as you planned?"

"You know the answer. You lied on me."

"I did what you did."

"Lied?"

"No, I kept a secret. Some secrets are worth keeping." I tried to move past him, but he cut me off again. "Look, we can become really good friends, Kimberly. I can teach you things and help you." He walks up closer to me, "Aren't you curious?" He rubbed the back of his hand across my breast, and I pushed him.

"Now, Kimmie. We are not going to do anything you don't want to. But don't you want a man's hand to grab you and touch you?"

"No!"

"You only say that because you don't know. I can teach you things, Kimmie." I started to circle around him as I backed away. As soon as I saw a clear path, I ran into my room and locked my door. He knocks at the door and says, "You can't stay in there forever. You got to eat."

"I'm good."

"So you aren't going to eat dinner either?"

"Naw."

"I will let your mother know; you said you didn't want to eat. No problem." He leaves from in front of my door, and I let my head fall on my desk, tears rolling down my face. I felt in my heart I could not live like this.

My mom came home hours later, and she didn't bother to come to my room to check on me. She believed whatever lie Greg told, and I got no dinner that night.

I was a prisoner in my own home.

Today is the day I decided not to come home. If my mom is tripping and her dude is a pervert, I shouldn't have to be there unless she is there. I just need somewhere to hide out until she gets home. I can't ask Ariana; that would be weird. Maybe I can hang with Raymond.

The bell rang, and I skipped the bus. The walk home is a bit long, but what else do I have to do? I started walking, and there he was, Raymond.

"Hey, you want me to walk with you home?"

"I'm not going home."

"Okay, so you want company for wherever you are going?"

"I don't know where I am going."

"Well, can you stop walking so fast, girl," he says jokingly. I slowed down, and he jogged up to me. "So what are you going to do?"

"I was just walking to burn some time."

"You want to go to the park?"

"Yeah, sure." We headed to the park and sat on the swings. It was fun to just get away from everything. Raymond was so easy to talk to. Why can't everyone else be this easy? He asked if I wanted to go to his house, but I wasn't sure what to say.

"I mean, if you don't want to go home, you can hang out with me. I am getting hungry." I was starving because I hadn't eaten. Lunch was terrible today, too, so I agreed. We sat at his kitchen island, ate the sandwiches he made, and drank juice. His hospitality for a middle-schooler was good.

"So, why don't you want to go home?"

"It's nothing."

"Nobody avoids going home because of nothing. So, is your mom tripping? Daddy issues?"

"I guess daddy issues."

"Maybe you should talk to him. Sometimes dads think differently."

"But what if my dad is the problem?"

"Tell your mom."

"And if she doesn't believe you?"

"Dang."

"Yeah, he isn't my real dad, but a creep my mom is dating."

"You need me to do something?"

"What are you going to do?"

He stands up from the stool and says, "Tell

him, hey, you need to be easy on my friend. She's a cool girl, and I don't like how you treating her."

I started laughing because I knew dang well that no middle schooler was going to talk to an adult like that. I wished he could have, though. "Yeah, if only you could talk like that."

"You know, Kimmie, I can protect my woman."

"I am your woman?"

"Yeah, I mean, we are going out, right?"

"Yeah, I mean, umm–yeah."

"Okay, then I should protect you when you need me."

"Right. So if I get into a fight, you going to fight for me?"

"Only if you are fighting a boy. If you going against a girl, my mom said, I can't hit women."

"Even if they try to fight you?"

"I am to avoid them at all costs. I would run from a girl, not because I am afraid. I don't want my momma to fight me. She is slick, scary. So hey, you are going to have to leave soon. My mom will be here, and you cannot be here."

I got up from the stool and thanked him for the food. I knew it couldn't last all day, but I tried to make it last as long as possible. We walked to the door, and he hugged me. But this time, he kissed me on the lips and said, "Bye," as he sheepishly walked back into the house. When I looked out to walk, I saw my mom, and my eyes were huge.

I ran across the street before she could start yelling at me and quickly got into her car. "Kimmie, so that is what you are doing now? Skipping school to hang out with boys?"

"No, mom. I was just walking home."

"No, you skipped taking the bus home and have been out here for hours. Were you at his house this whole time?"

"No, mom."

"I am out here looking for you, and I find you walking out of a boy's house and him giving you a kiss on the mouth. I don't believe you. You better not let me catch you talking to this boy ever again."

"But mom–"

"What!! —-- he is your boyfriend, Kimmie?! You can't have a boyfriend; you are a child."

"We were just at the park and came here to get something to eat."

"There is food at home."

"But Greg is at home."

"Look, you and Greg need to work this out tonight. You don't have any business in a boy's house. Greg said you would be doing something like this, and I didn't believe him. If I hadn't seen it with my own eyes, I wouldn't have believed him. I started to think maybe he was lying."

"You don't think he is lying?"

"No, he said you have been locked in your room chatting with boys."

194

"Boys!"

"Yeah, you either ignore him at home, or you lock yourself in your room."

"Yes, I ignore him, and no, I don't like being around him."

"I wasn't going to tell you this until I felt you were ready. But honey, Greg and I got engaged a few days ago. I wanted you two to connect more, so I gave you guys a chance to talk. But Kimmie, we are getting married in November."

"In three months?"

"We have been dating for over a year, going on two. I think he is going to be helpful with me knowing what to do with you. He has a daughter, and you and Ariana get along well."

"I love Ariana, but I hate her father."

"I don't expect you to like all of my decisions, but this one you are going to have to live with, Kimmie. I pick who I marry, and I would like you to respect him even if you don't like him."

I said nothing as I stared forward. Why do things keep piling on when you think you are having a good day? I gritted my teeth, and I stared out the window. We pull up in the driveway, and Greg comes out the door. "Hey, where have you been? I called your phone and tried to reach you. I helped your mom track your phone."

"So you guys are following me?"

"Yup, we had to make sure you were safe, Kimmie." He patted me on the shoulder as I walked past him. "Thanks, Greg," my mom said to him as I walked further ahead. Then she said to him, "I told her."

"How did she take it?"

"She wasn't happy, but I told her she will have to get used to you being part of this family." They both trailed after me into the house. I volunteered to be grounded to my room, so my mom brought me my food with Greg looking on from the doorway. He felt like a dark spot that was hovering or a rain cloud that wouldn't go away. He made faces at me while my mother's back was turned, and I started to dislike my mother strongly.

At school the next day, when I saw Raymond, he asked to talk to me. We were outside for P.E. when he asked, "So what happened yesterday when I saw your mom?"

"Yeah, they tracked my phone."

"Oh, you good?"

"Kind of. She said I can't see you anymore."

"Well, she's not in school. He leans over and kisses her on the lips."

"Hey, can you not do that."

"What? You don't want me to kiss you?"

"No, I mean, yes, but not now."

"So you want me to kiss you, or you don't?"

"I like you, Raymond, but I don't want to be kissing."

"So then you don't like me."

"No, I do, I just–"

"Look, don't worry about it." Raymond turns to walk away, and I grab him and say, "Where are you going? I thought we were talking?"

"We just did." He turned his back and started to walk to the guys waiting for him. He says back to me, "Hey, by the way, you ain't my girl no more." I stood there near the bleachers, confused and embarrassed. Why did he dump me? Worse was to follow when I had to deal with what he told his friends about me.

How could I have been so stupid and been around him by myself? It wasn't an hour later that I started seeing people eyeball me. Going to third period, Ariana came up to me and said, "Hey, do you know what people are saying about you?"

"No, what?"

"They are saying you had sex with Raymond, and you both were caught kissing at the bleachers."

"What? He kissed me at the bleachers, and I told him to stop. He just broke up with me."

"Did you have sex with him?"

"Sex, we never even talked about it. I only kissed him on the cheek, and he kissed me twice."

"That's not what the school heard."

"Oh my God." I walked into the third period, wishing to fade into the background. Ariana was not as chill as I was. As soon as Raymond came into the classroom, she went up to him. "Why are you out here lying about my sister?"

"About what?"

"You know what you said, and now you better tell the truth!"

The teacher pokes her head back into the classroom and says, "Quiet down, sit down. We are going to get started in a minute." Our teacher was in the hallway talking to the other teacher, which meant Raymond had about a minute to fess up.

"I ain't lie about nothing. Your sister isn't as innocent as you all think she is. We kissed, and yesterday we–" Ariana grabbed him with his arm and body-slammed him before he could say another word. He tried to get her off of him but failed. Every kick or punch he tried couldn't land.

The teacher came in to break up the commotion. "Ariana, Raymond, come with me." The three of them went down to the principal's office. It was about thirty minutes before they called me there, too. The class joined in a choir of "oooh." I knew this was about the rumor. All I could pray was that they would not call my mom.

I got to the office, and they asked me a series of questions about sex and my behavior. It was awkward, and I honestly didn't listen. Until they said, "We are going to call your mother about today."

"No, please don't call my mother. She is out sick, and my stepdad, Greg, is watching me."

"We have to check and see if he is on your emergency contact list."

"Let me call him. I think he is." I called the only person I could think to get me out of this, and I wasn't sure if I should go with the devil. I know compared to my mom, the raging dragon, he was the best option. I knew I could live another day after this school scandal. He answered the phone, and I asked him to come get me. He didn't hesitate to call the school back.

I was in the car with Greg, headed home. Ariana's mom was called before they realized her father was on the way to the school to pick me up. She left before me. I wasn't sure if Greg planned that, to miss seeing Ariana and his ex-wife leaving the school's parking lot.

Inside the car, he asked, "So, you didn't leave that boy alone, did you?" I didn't reply to him because this was one of the moments where his talking was rhetorical and had nothing to do with getting an honest answer. This fake teaching moment made me want to puke.

"Didn't I tell you young boys only want one thing from a girl like you?"

I kept looking out the window, and I said nothing.

"Are you going to at least tell me thank you?"

"No."

"I have another way you can thank me." The comment sent the hairs standing up on my arms and legs. He was so creepy, and I hated being near him. Pulling up in the driveway was beyond uncomfortable. I got to the door and tried to rush inside to my room, but he took me by my hand before I could. He swung me back onto the couch.

"Now, why are you off so quickly? We have plenty of time to talk and get to know each other before your mom comes." He started kissing me on my neck, and the wet kisses were disgusting. If I disliked kisses from Raymond, there was no way I wanted wet ones from my mom's soon-to-be devil husband. I felt like his hands were all over my body, and I wanted to crawl away, but he pinned me.

His right hand was trying to go under my shirt when the door opened. I felt someone jump on his back, and he stumbled up to his feet. He was being choked from behind, and little fists kept hitting him. After he got off what was like a cat from his back, he stared his daughter in the face.

"Dad, what the fuck?"

"Don't use that language with me."

"Dad, you are disgusting. Why are you doing this?"

"It's not what you think."

"Really? I just saw you groping on your stepdaughter. What is your problem?" And then she looked at me, "Why didn't you say anything?"

Embarrassed, I shrugged my shoulders because I didn't know why I didn't tell her. I guess I thought she wouldn't believe me, too. She looks back to her father, "I am calling the cops."

"Baby, don't do that. Come on, I am your dad."

"No, you are just a piece of shit that tried to rape my sister!"

"Now, you know I wouldn't do that. Have I ever done anything to you?"

"Maybe because you didn't have the chance. Or because you are my father!"

200

"Look, if you do this, they are going to make me go on a list. She would have to go to court and confess this in front of everyone. You too."

"I don't care who I need to talk to; you need to go to jail." While the two of them are arguing, I am already calling the police and praying they hear the noise in the background. I know if I put it to my face, he will snatch it away. I was crying and shaking because I wasn't sure how this would end.

The police did come to the house because I am guessing they heard the two of them arguing for the next five minutes. The lights shining through the window scared the hell out of him. He looked at me and said, "You Bitch, call the dame police!"

I said nothing, and he came charging toward me. As soon as the police got into the house and saw that he was near me, they tased him. This was the first time I was beyond happy to see the police. Ariana backed up away from them and let them do their job of carrying his butt out of the house. They said they would need to file a report and understand everything that had happened.

My mom was called, and she got to the house quickly. They asked her several questions, and she denied having any idea that her soon-to-be husband was a pedophile. She sure knew how to pick them. I didn't want to stay with her anymore, and I was sure to tell the cops that.

I asked Ariana if I could leave the house with her because I couldn't stay with my mom. She just made me sick. She didn't love me but only did what she had to do to care for me, not protect me. I was done with giving her chances, and on that day. If this was her best, I was better off alone.

I stayed with Ariana for a few days before the

lady from the school came to talk to me. She knew about what happened and asked if I wanted to go home. I told her, "No, I don't want to live there anymore." She told me she knew how I felt and that she would make sure that I was safe. She tried to talk to my dad, but he had a small room in a rehabilitation ward, which he just gave up on trying to get out of.

When my dad found out what had happened, he just spent the time crying. I told him it wasn't his fault, but he repeatedly blamed himself for not being there. He went on about how he was cursed. Everyone close to him gets hurt. I don't know how something about me ended up becoming about him and death.

Clearly, I couldn't move in with my dad. I knew it, and so did the nice lady. Even if he had money, his mental competence wasn't sufficient to care for me anymore. He was broken, and there was nothing I could do to help him. What can you really do to heal a broken heart?

Surprisingly, everything at school died down about Raymond and I. Some of the other boys tried to talk to me, probably thinking I was fast, and my ride-or-die sister threatened them all. Even though mom's wedding was off, Ariana never stopped being there for me. She is the type of sister any girl needs in her life. I just wished we could have lived together.

The first assigned home I stayed in was a joke. They were clearly about the money and could give two red cents about what happened to me unless that meant the money would stop. She had about four or five children that she cared for. We were all fending for ourselves for food, and often, I would go hungry.

I don't know if my expectations were just too high, but I never ate box meals at home. My mom either ordered out or made a real meal with real food. This woman buys anything in a box or from a store's frozen section and warms it up. She never takes us anywhere or buys us a thing. Even though I get money every week, she takes it all and puts it on herself.

She eats well while we eat whatever we can scrape together from her fragmented fridge. I hated this house and couldn't wait for the nice lady to come back and move me somewhere else. I stayed with that home until I had finished sixth grade. Going to seventh grade, my mom tried to get me to come back and promised that things would be different. I just couldn't believe her.

My memory couldn't shake how I felt living with her. While my life might appear worse, it was better to be mistreated by strangers than your own kin–and definitely your own mother. The second house was just as crazy. I mean, are these people just lying on their applications? How is there a huge disconnect between my experience and what I was told?

The nice lady told me this house would be better, but it was worse. This second house lady bought me things, but the other girls would steal my stuff, and she did nothing about it. She cooked, but she didn't really care about our everyday stuff. I think she was mostly overwhelmed by what we each needed.

I get it. There are a lot of children in the system, but why do these families take on so many children if they can't properly support them? If I ever grow up to adopt or foster, I would never do this. That year living with that family was full of ups and downs, and it taught me how to be scrappy.

I didn't have street smarts at all until I spent that year with that family. I learned I had to provide for myself. I knew as soon as I could I was getting a job to take care of myself. I didn't want to rely on the system or people to take care of me like this. Maybe I got that from my mother.

The third house I went to was the home of another teenager, Derrick. This guy was a proper butthole and didn't care how he treated anyone. I hated being around him so much. I tried anything I could to get out of the house and have less of a reason to be there.

I tried enrolling in sports, playing chess, and even cheerleading. I was at a loss on what to do until Ariana told me one day to go to church! "Can you imagine? Me going to church?" She told me, "You tried everything else, so why not try Jesus? Ain't that what they say?"

She didn't come with me to church but pointed me in the direction of someone who went faithfully, Kayda. She was a young girl who was like a little minister. She read the Bible on the bus to school, and she often sat alone or with her bestie, Christian. She was always bubbly and kind. I introduced myself to her and asked, "Hey, do you go to church?"

"Yes, I love church. It is like my second home. Do you?"

"No, but I was thinking about going."

"Oh, well, you can come with me to my church. Will you need a ride?"

"Yeah, I would."

"Okay, well, let me get your number, and I will help you get a ride."

"Of course, yeah, thanks." I gave her my number, and the girl worked like a secretary. It was nice to meet someone who was genuinely nice. I hated that I overlooked her last year and mostly this year, too. I was heading to eighth grade, my final year of middle school, and I needed a break.

I realized that I might have needed prayer to change my life. I went to church with her that weekend. Walking into that church, I instantly felt lighter. I don't know what it was that made me feel different. Was it the smiles from adults and children? Was it the song played on the piano or the sermon that hooked me?

That day, a guest speaker, Dr. Krystal Lee, was there. She was up speaking about how it rains on the just and the unjust. She said it is normal to expect the rain, but nobody expects it to downpour.

Funny enough, I could understand what she was talking about. She was talking about how we all have a story, and no life is perfect, no matter how it looks on the outside.

"If you right now feel like the cares of life are beating you down one after another. I want you to know the pressure can be eased, the burden can be made light, and the yoke you feel around your neck leading you to chaos can be removed." This little lady didn't run up and down the stage but walked the floor and spoke casually. I was invested in her talk.

She then said, "If you are here, and you know you need a release, I want you to raise your hand." I heard her, and I knew I should have raised my hand, but I didn't. I sat there quietly. I didn't want people to know me like that. But she asked again, and this time, she pointed to me.

I looked behind me, thinking she was speaking to someone else, but she pointed to me and said, "I am talking to you, beautiful. Come here for a second." I got up from my seat and walked up to her. She passed the mic to someone else, and she whispered in my ear.

"Can you hear me?" I nodded my head yes. "I want you to do me a favor. If what I am saying to you makes sense, I want you to raise both of your hands above your head." I nodded. She started to pray,

"Father, in the mighty name of Yashua, I come to you today right now concerning your daughter. You pointed her out, and you said you wanted to release a Word to her and I am only being obedient. Daughter, I know today you are not where you should be, and where you were is a place you cannot return. I commend you for making the choice to stand on your own two feet, even if that means standing alone."

She continues to speak, "Thank you for honoring your mother even when most would say you couldn't. You have been an example of strength, and I am pursuing you. I want you to know, no matter what it looks like, I am right here with you. I am building you, molding you, and I will always give you a way of escape. No matter what obstacles come, if you trust me, I will open a door for you every time."

She looks at me intently and says, "If you need rest, He says He is here for you. If you need strength, I Am. If you need clothes, food, shelter, or anything else, just ask Me. You have the ear of God listening to you, and He says He is concerned about you. Wow."

My arms were lifted high above my head. I don't know how this little lady could tell me so much without saying much, but whatever this was that was speaking to me, I had to get closer to it. I needed this hug. I needed to know this God. I wanted Him in my life, and only I knew how much.

I felt a hand go on the small of my back and another on my stomach. My head fell down forward, and I could only hear the lady praying, "Young lady, do you want God to come into your life and be your guide to help you?"

"Yes."

"Okay, now we are going to repent and ask for salvation. Would you like that?"

"Yes--but I am not all sure what it means."

"I am going to walk you through this. This

prayer is to ask Yah, God, to help you know what is right and wrong. He will become your guide and foundation for what you believe is right or wrong. Does that make sense?"

I nod my head yes.

"Repeat after me. Father, in the name of Yashua, we believe that you are the Word born in the flesh. That you are the One that heals, saves, and delivers. That you are concerned, willing, and able to save this young lady from every sin, either past, present, or future. We ask now for you to come into her heart, to dwell within her, guide her, and show her Your way.

We cast down every other thought that would have us believe that our way is better than yours but yield our spirit to your teaching. I will commit to following Your Word, commands, and make Your truth the foundation for my life. Okay, good."

I echoed every word she said. When she prayed, I felt lighter. She had this more to say, "May You fill her with Your Holy Spirit and keep her all the days of her life. In the mighty name of Yashua, Jesus the Christ, we say hallelujah, and so be it."

She gave my hands a squeeze, and I gave her a hug. She told me she would speak to me after service, and she did. She was such a nice lady, and she scared me a little bit because she knew so much stuff. I could tell her my whole life if she allowed me to, but she silenced me and said, "Yah knows everything. I am just a messenger. But I want you to pray; talk to Him, just like I am talking to you now. And if you got a phone, get a bible app and start reading scriptures."

I listened to everything she said, and I did it.

I started reading my bible like the girl on the bus. I could listen to radio talk shows about teaching for hours. This introduction helped me in a big way. I came to every service they had, and Mrs. Bell liked me a lot. She was like the church mother.

She knew everybody's children, their family names, and history. I enjoyed listening to her talk. She would talk for a long time about things she remembered growing up. I enjoyed hearing her out and comparing the prices of things from then to now. She had one daughter. But her daughter was grown and out living her life. She said she raised her grandchild, but she wasn't on speaking terms with her daughter because it was her choice.

I would visit her house every day, and one day, she asked, "How would you feel if I adopted you?

"Really? You want to adopt a teenager?"

"Yeah, why not?"

"Because most people like babies to adopt. They may need you more."

"That's kind of you, but what if I felt like I needed you? Would you be okay with that?"

"I mean, yes. I would love that."

"I will work on the paperwork and see what happens."

It was a quick conversation that could have changed my life. She went through the proper channels but didn't get too far. They didn't think, based on her age, it would be a good fit. She was ninety years old, and they worried about the stress I could cause her with me being a teenager. My mom was also not being helpful; she was still trying to get me to move back with her and wasn't ready to see me adopted by anyone.

So she didn't adopt me but said I could come and stay with her as often as I liked. She even gave me a key to her house! I came to her house every day after school. I slept over there more than I did at my foster parent's house. She didn't care because she was getting the check and had one less mouth to feed.

Things were going great. I was happy. I came to see my dad and told him about the great news. He was grateful, but the look in his eyes still seemed far away. It was like I couldn't win with him. If I was sad, he was sadder. When I was glad, he grew sad still because he wasn't part of it.

Dad wanted to save me. I told him he didn't have to because God saved me already. He burst into tears, and all I could think of was to give him a hug. He asked me to pray with him, and I did.

I remember one day getting back from school to Mrs. Bell's house. I got a call from my foster mom. "Hey, I just got a call for you to call the place for your dad." I thanked her for the message, hung up, and called the home where my dad was staying.

"Hello, I was calling about my dad, Gerald James."

"Yes, we have an update about your father, and we would like to see you in person."

"Okay, is everything alright?"

"There was an accident at the center, and we want to speak with you." I hung up the phone, and

I went straight there. They welcomed me and my grandma, who was also there. They thanked us both for coming and brought us to our father's room, where they had a box.

Nobody told us about his accident when it happened. Apparently, they were leaving messages with my grandma, who never checks her voicemail. My dad had gotten into a serious accident a few days before, and he was hit by a car. As my grandmother and I sat there on his bed, the lady gave us the box and said we could keep anything else in the room we wanted for him.

Over the years, he had tons of things there, but not all of them we wanted to keep. He only had his clothes and things we had to pack up for him. I asked my grandma what happened, and she explained. He was sitting in his wheelchair looking outside. They're not sure how a gear in his chair malfunctioned, and he rolled into the street into oncoming traffic.

I could see how this was impacting my grandma. I was certain she was not going to be safe after. She lost her only son and husband. It was just she and I, and I hadn't seen her much because of the mental breakdown she had after the death of my grandfather. I was scared for her. She had no one to help her through this because I was too young to be of any real help.

I took several things to remind me of my dad. Later that night, I cried, and I cried. I was grateful that Mrs. Bell offering to come with me to the funeral. Her granddaughter was a jerk about it.

"Grandma, why are you going to the funeral? She is not your family."

"Little girl, I don't need you telling me who is

and is not my family."

"But think about it, Grandma. This girl comes into your life, and all she does is get money from you. You better be sure this is real before you keep forking over money."

"You mean like I do with you? You only come around when you want something."

"Grandma, I am really hurt," she says sarcastically. "We are family; you are my grandmother."

"Yes, I am, and I am her mother."

"But the adoption didn't go through."

"Some adoptions are in the heart. I don't need any paper to tell me that. Now come on; let's go." The ladies head out to the funeral. Mrs. Bell's granddaughter, Jessica, was always rude and feisty towards me. I didn't understand it, though. She had the woman I only recently met and am getting to know all of her life. If I had a grandmother like her, I couldn't be moved no matter how hard people tried to disrespect her.

Mrs. Bell was a gem. Yes, she was old. I think she was like ninety-five. But she was so full of life. She said what she meant and made no apologies. She was kind to help with funeral costs for my dad. She never said how much she gave, but I was grateful. My mom did show up, and I was surprised. It was nice to see her briefly and give her a hug. She seemed broken up about a few things when I saw her.

I don't hate her, and I was glad to get that off my chest when I saw her. I think she needed to hear it just as much as I wanted to say it. We needed to clear the air, and that was done. That night was a lonely night. I realized I really didn't have anyone left who understood me from my family. I had no choice but to create the family God wanted me to have.

Mrs. Bell was a huge support for me during the death of my father and this realization. I offered to get a job on my next birthday. I know some companies allow you to work when you turn fifteen. I had been living with her for over a year, and she never mentioned money. She bought my clothes, food, and anything I needed. Jessica also made sure to point it out.

She told me to come here and sit next to her, and I did. "I want you to hear me well. I don't need a piece of paper to prove you are my daughter. Children are not only the ones you birth but the ones that are in your heart. You are in my heart, Kimberly, and I will always be here for you."

"After my dad died, it just feels like I don't have anybody."

"Don't believe that lie from the devil. You are not alone. God Almighty is with you. I am here for you. And even my knuckle-headed daughter is here for you, too. Don't let her try and scare you off. She has what is hers, and there is still more. Just be yourself and let God use you."

I gave this woman a hug who has quickly become a part of my life. She continued to say, "And don't think you don't have a momma; you hear me?" I nodded in agreement. "You don't know what all a mother goes through for their children. She isn't perfect, but that doesn't mean you throw her away. You pray for her. Because she needs you. Someday, you will see how you need her, too."

The woman was wise and had a way with

words. That year was hard losing my dad, but it was so much easier because I had her in my corner. We sometimes also talked about my mom, and she kept telling me I couldn't run from her forever. The truth is, I wanted to. I didn't want to have to deal with her anymore. I honestly felt done.

But she was right; my mom did bring me here, and the Bible talks about loving here and forgiveness. I ain't going to lie. This process is going to take me longer than a year. I am not sure what it will take for me to get over the craziness, but I am trying.

Finishing eighth grade was not hard. I was really good in English, writing, math, and science. I passed with flying colors. I looked forward to college if it would be like this. I wasn't totally sure of what I wanted to do, but I knew starting a business would be ideal. One day, a few months after my dad had passed, we got some unexpected mail.

There was a letter written out to me, and it was from an insurance company. I opened the letter, and I almost passed out, but I found out that my dad had a life insurance policy. I was a beneficiary listed with my grandmother. He left 70% of the award to me and 30% to his mother. I held the letter, stunned. My dad, even from the grave, was trying to look out for me.

They didn't rule his death as a suicide because it didn't appear that he intentionally wheeled himself into traffic. The break they now believe malfunctioned because the fight my grandmother made about his death being ruled a suicide initially was overturned, and we won!

I wasn't able to access the money until I was eighteen, but it was breathtaking to find out I had it. The unfortunate part is that my foster mom found out I had it, too. She wanted to adopt me because it looked like I was living with her, and things were great; she started the paperwork without me knowing about it. There was a clause that my guardian could use a portion of the money to care for me if need be in his will.

I knew she only wanted to adopt me because of the money, and I refused to allow her to do that. I knew that leaving her house also meant I couldn't stay with Mrs. Bell anymore. I was now 14. She said I had to leave her house because she was heartbroken about my refusal for her to adopt me–a bunch of lies. They decided to put me in a group home. I just need to survive two years there, and I will file to be emancipated and do what I want.

High School

The process began, and my first year of high school was filled with uncertainty. Going into the group home was a bit scary and lonely. The girls oftentimes called me *dumb* because I chose to be away from my family when others were trying to get back home.

They just didn't understand. I wasn't going to become an open book for others to validate my choice. At the end of the day, it was my choice. I had a right to choose how I lived my life, and I wasn't given power to a kid I barely knew.

"Alright, Girls, quiet down. It is lights out, and I need you all to go to bed. I don't want to see bad grades because you are not getting your rest. If you need me, I am down the hall." The night clerk left the dorm and went down the hall. As soon as her feet retracted, the same girl seemed to talk the same trash every night.

"That dumb bitch. Does she really think any of us are going to bed? Ain't nobody going to bed.

Who wants to watch tv on my phone?" said Shanice, one of the older girls. She was seventeen and in the eleventh grade going on the tenth. I am not sure if she is dumb or if she does it on purpose. I think she tries to stay here because she is afraid of the outside world. Who fails tenth grade three times?

She was either dumb or extremely distracted. The way she talked about people made you think she had all the senses and was some kind of baddie. She is a girl with bad acne, a bad attitude, is rude, and she talks too much. But maybe I am harsh? But I doubt it.

It took everything in me not to tell her to shut up when she started yapping. A few of the other girls would gather around her and allow her stupidity to impregnate their thoughts, too. I refused to be one of them. One night, I saw shadows near my dresser. "Hey, what are you doing?"

She was rummaging through my stuff, and I caught her. From my bed I said, "Look, get away from my stuff!"

"Hey, calm down; all the girls in here share."

"Okay, that is nice. I just don't want to share my clothes. They have sentimental value." She threw my clothes down on the floor.

"Oh, I thought my stuff was at the bottom of the drawer." I got out of my bed, and her friends got up to stand with her. "Like I said, we share here. Do you mind if I use your shirt tomorrow? I saw you wear it, and it's kind of cute."

I didn't answer her, but I laid back down on my bed with death in my eyes. One thing I learned about a bully is that you cannot win every battle, but if you calculate, you can win the war. I have eighteen more months to go. I needed to buy some time. The girls dispersed, but not after a few of my garments took a walk.

I have one thing most of the girls here don't: money. I took the bus and went to see Mrs. Bell. I told her about what happened, and she told me she would drop me off there. She bought me a case with a key lock. I wasn't going to let these girls rob me blind.

They saw me put my case down on the floor, and some of them smacked their lips. If you want to put a mark on your back, the fastest way to do it is to show others you have money or help. I put my headphones on when I was in the common area, and at night, I would leave my technology in the office. I knew there was nothing they would love more than to break my phone or crack my headphones.

The silent war inside of the group home was started…

Chapter 18

At school, the same girls would try to torment me by kicking my shoes or trying to trip me in the halls. They hated that I was smart and I had no intentions of living off the system. I was on the fast track to emancipation, and Ariana and I talked about it a lot. We ended up going to the same high school, and it was so good to see a familiar face.

"If I was you, I would just go crazy one time and start laying them out. All you need is one good fight to scare the other ones. None of them really want to fight you, but one. Fight the one who wants the fight, or fight one well enough so the others don't want to fight."

"You sound crazy, Ariana. You sure you don't watch too many movies?"

"I watch a lot of London films, and I got to tell you, fights solve some of your problems."

"You know I am a believer, so fighting is like the last resort for me. I am trying to kill this with kindness, but the girls are pushing me. They try to steal my stuff, take my clothes, and somebody put lipstick in my clothes and ruined all my whites."

"Girl, you may have to stop being so nice."

"I will keep that in mind. You know the plan."

"Yeah, hang out for two years and emancipate yourself. Girl, that is a long time away." She was right. It was a long time to make it with these miniature spawns of Satan. Shanice came by just in time to slap down my books, "Yo, what you do that for? Do you have a problem?" I came up to Ariana, "No, no, don't do that. It's cool."

"Yeah, Kimmie, you need to get your friend."

"Look, you don't know me. But I know where you live."

"Is that supposed to scare me?"

"If I got my father locked up, I won't shed a tear to see your dumbass get what you got coming to you."

"Say that to my face." I pulled Ariana away and went the other way. The teachers started to come out into the hallway because children knew how to start a commotion in the midst of switching classes. I know she thinks she is helping, but it really was making my life worse.

"Girl, you gotta chill."

"Naw, she needs to know ain't nobody scared of her. She is the only person up in here who likely won't graduate until she is twenty-five. This isn't a four-year university. Get your edumacation and get the hell on." Ariana and I were really good at laughing together. Her dad ended up going to jail, but the time he got wasn't long enough. He got two years and would likely get out in a few more months on good behavior. That's the system for you.

Ariana and I had three classes together, but in P.E. and my last period, I was on my own. The worst two times to be without a good friend. The best part was that P.E. was just before my last class. So, after working out, I could be stinky if I needed to be and head home. I hated using the showers at school. I felt like anyone of them could either be staring at me or trying to frame me; either way, it wasn't happening.

In the locker room, Shanice couldn't help herself, "If your friend keeps running her mouth, I might have to lay some hands on her."

"Yeah, she can handle herself."

"But what if I wanted to fight you?" Shanice got in my way, and I walked around her.

"I ain't got no problems with you."

"You sure about that?"

Without looking at her, I walked away. But she wasn't satisfied, and I felt a huge thrust pushing me forward. My shoes weren't slippery, so I didn't fall forward. "What the hell is your problem?"

"There she is. So you got some heart, Kimmie?"

"I don't have time for people like you. Likely, you are gonna be on the first thang smoking to a female prison, and I am not wasting my life on you!"

"Ohh, okay, we got jokes. You don't talk like that when we are at home?"

"Not the time."

"How about now?" She swings, and I step

back. I thought, at any moment, someone would walk through the door because that normally happens right in the movies, but nobody came in. That's when it hit me; she told them all to stay out. "Look, I ain't trying to fight you."

"Because you scared?"

"No, I don't believe violence solves real problems. I think a conversation can help resolve this."

"You think you better than us, don't you?"

"No, I think you believe I am better than you. Who am I to disagree?"

"You see that right there is why I don't like you. You have a smart-ass mouth. She swung again but in the other direction, and I moved just in time for her to hit her hand on the bathroom door. "Shit." She started holding her hand and saying some more curse words as I walked out of the bathroom into the open space of the locker room.

These girls ain't about nothing. They are either jealous, stupid followers, or have no backbone. I am not losing my future for fighting some dumb girls who don't care if they lose it all because they don't have much to lose. I do. A fight like this will get me expelled and make me look bad on paper.

I wanted to go see Mrs. Bell. She had been sick the last few days. She had health problems, but nothing more than what every other adult her age, I am sure, was facing. She was conscious about what she ate. So I figured she would live a long time.

But I kept calling because it wasn't like her not to call me back. When she didn't reply after a week, I started calling the hospitals. If she didn't have her phone, that would be the only reason she wouldn't call me. I am sure her mean daughter had something to do with that. After calling four hospitals, I found her.

I got on the first city bus heading to her hospital, and surprisingly enough, they allowed me to visit her. She was sleeping when I first came in. I grabbed her by her hand and didn't say a word. I didn't want to disturb her, but I guess she could tell it was me.

She woke up, squeezed my hand, and said, "I knew you would come."

"Of course. How long have you been here?"

"About a week or two. I am not sure. The day and the night look the same."

"Why have you been here for so long?"

"They say I have some kind of blood thing. They are running tests, but my platelets are dropping, and they are not sure why. They are saying I may have to do a procedure weekly just to keep them elevated."

"That sounds like a lot."

"It is, and I ain't doing it."

"But mom, you have to follow what they say."

"No, I don't. I have a God in heaven that can heal me."

"But Mom, what if that doesn't happen?"

"Then it is my time to go."

"But why–"

"How's school? Them girls being nice to you now?"

"No, mom. They still mean. It is one girl that stirs the nest."

"Yeah, we all have a thorn in our side, don't we?"

"You're a smart girl, and a lot of girls will be jealous of you."

"But Mom, I don't see why? I got what they got right now. We all live in the same place. A few shirts doesn't make someone better than you."

"Some people are like that."

"Do you think you will get out of here soon?"

"I don't know, but we will see what the Good Lord permits." She starts to drift to sleep.

"Grandma, I gotta get on the bus to make curfew." She opens her eyes and says, "Okay, yes, baby, of course. Come pray with me before you leave. Father in heaven, please keep my daughter safe as she travels back home. Give her mercy and grace as she goes, and keep her forever in Your presence. I am thankful for her and for You being the healer and the savior of my life. May You keep us both in Your precious hands, in Jesus' name. Amen."

"I love you mom."

"I love you more." I embraced her one more time, and her warmth seemed to linger on me. Leaving the hospital, I felt lighter, and the prayer seemed to have done something. When I got to the center, the girls were staring at me as I walked in. It looked like Shanice had to wrap her hand after her stupid decision to punch a bathroom door. Maybe that will teach her a lesson.

I went to the room and started getting my nightly routine together. I tried my best to get there in just enough time to get ready to go to bed whenever I could. I showered, brushed my teeth, and put up my hair. The night thus far was uneventful.

But getting in the bed that night, something didn't feel right. I wasn't sure what it was, but something wasn't right. I had never heard a voice from God in my life, but that night, I could hear a voice telling me in my head not to go to sleep. So I lay in my bed for about an hour.

And I could feel the girls moving in, and at that moment, I heard Him say, "Roll." I rolled out of the bed and ended up on the floor. I started kicking and screaming under the bed. I felt a few hands trying to grab me, and I screamed all the more.

The hands disappeared, and the lights turned on. The night lady came in and started looking frantically for the noise. She looked under the bed and said, "Are you alright? Get up, girl, and stop dreaming! You are going to wake up the entire room!"

I pretended to be asleep and woke up startled at her voice. I quickly got up from under the bed, and I asked her, "I am sorry, but I may toss and turn all night. Can I get some water or something?"

"You know everything is locked down."

"But if I don't get out of this room and I go back to sleep, I may scream again. I am having nightmares."

"Okay, you can get a glass of water, and that

is it."

"Fine. Thank you."

I walked out of the room with the lady, and she gave me a drink of water. She sat there and watched me sip slowly. It was a good night to be up because I threw out a simple comment that the Lord prompted, and she started singing like a canary.

We talked for about thirty minutes, and she walked me back to the room. I wasn't sure if everyone was sleeping, but they knew I was going to call out if there was an issue. They all stayed in their beds that night. But I knew it was a matter of time before they might try it again. The next time, I will be ready for them.

I was up early. I skipped my shower that day because I didn't trust being around them. I will birdbath at school before I trust any of them. I also skipped the gym, in that I didn't dress down, and I got a zero for the day. I approached the teacher after class and explained I was having menstrual cramps. He said this was the only one-time excuse he was giving me.

I was relieved and wished that Ariana was there that day to talk to her, but she wasn't. Only one person could make this day better for me: Mrs. Bell. I tried to call her cell, but there was no answer. She's old school, so I called the house and she answered.

"Hey, Kimmie."

"Hi, Mom, how are you?"

"Doing alright. I won't complain."

"If there were something going on, you would tell me, right?"

226

"Yes, baby girl, if I felt that was best."

"How are things at school and with the girls?"

"It's a bit crazy, if I am honest. I think they tried to jump me last night."

"Wait, really, what makes you so sure?"

"There was a gang of girls around my bed, and I heard God tell me to roll. I surprised them all, I am sure, when I went under the bed and started kicking and screaming."

"Shouldn't you report something like this?"

"It would be their words against mine. Plus, I didn't see any faces, although I could guess the ringleader."

"I am so sorry stuff like this is happening to good girls like you."

"Don't worry. I am going to get them back. I got a plan."

"Really?"

"Yup, if you have to bail me out of jail, just know I got them."

"Now, don't go doing nothing stupid."

"It won't be anything dumb, I promise. But they will leave me alone or want to kill me afterward." I started laughing, and although Mrs. Bell knew I was joking, a part of her knew I was also serious. We talked a bit more about the weather and small talk before I had to face the boss and then head to my room. I hated the rules in this place, but it sure beat staying with a creepy family.

Not all homes are bad. I was just one of the unlucky ones who kept getting poor placement. If I didn't see Mrs. Bell, I might have caved and went home after the last house, but God made a way. I realized as I sat in that group home it was more like a prison yard than a house for growing girls.

This was a place many of us landed because we couldn't get along with foster homes. In some of our cases like mine, we just had bad foster parents and were not the problem at all–perhaps the system is what is messed up the most. We don't get to choose who fosters us; we are just pushed like cattle through any open door. I was so ready for my birthday, that was days away.

I wondered, what would I do? I wasn't too crazy about asking for anything. Who would give it to me anyway? In here, you get twenty dollars, a card, and a cake if you are lucky. You get one quick trip to the mall. So you better know which store you want in advance. They don't like waiting around for you, and if you miss curfew, they file you as a runaway.

The rules were strict, but we are also on our last leg with the system. I guess some of us need a strong hand, and when these girls came knocking at my door again, I was determined to speak a language they all could understand. Somehow, I just knew they would plan something for my birthday, so I was on high alert that day.

It started off as a normal day. I knew I needed to shower today, so I paid one of the girls to switch places with me. I wasn't taking chances, and the price was cheap for my sanity, sweets. In here, money isn't how you get anything like in jail; you need stuff people could use, such as food and toiletries. I kept a stash of things in my locked case. Some of the girls knew. I tried my best to unload my goodies while the noisiest people were showering.

Mrs. Bell always managed to send me a box of goodies even if she didn't drop it off. They were picky about visitors, so mailing was the best option. We didn't always get a lift to the store either. Going to buy it yourself was out of the question. We got a weekly allowance of like ten dollars to buy anything we needed, including pads and tampons. It is a sad day to see someone choosing between menstrual products like pain management pills and tampons.

Thank goodness I wasn't on my period because as I left the shower, I felt someone push me from behind. And, of course, with no surprise, I heard Shanice say, "Isn't it your birthday today? Shouldn't we be giving you birthday licks or something?"

I didn't say a word but knew I needed to be at my towel and quickly. I got there and wrapped myself quickly and picked up the second towel as I backed up. "Look, I don't need this today. You don't either." Shanice was walking slowly up to me. The time she had waited for my birthday to come around gave her mangled hand time to heal.

"You didn't think we were finished, did you? I told you I was going to get you. Lucky you; I can give you your first present." When she retracted her fist to swing toward me, I pulled out my sock that had a soap bar in it.

I was holding on to this sock night and day because I knew she would try and think to have company. When the girls saw me yank out that sock and swing it, it landed on Shanice's face. It was as if you could hear the connection of the soap against her mouth make a pop! She grabbed her jaw, and some blood dribbled out onto the floor.

"Did you just knock out my tooth?"

I giggled at first because the whole situation was pathetic. "What do you mean? Of course, I didn't; you are just bleeding." But when I saw her hands come down, she had, in fact, lost a tooth. The bleeding got worse. She rushed into the bathroom to get a towel, and for a few seconds, it was as if she was in shock. She didn't start screaming until she looked in the mirror. I quickly exited the bathroom and finished getting changed.

She was either going to rat me out (I was ready for it), or she would make up a story to save face. The ones who saw it would know, and I didn't care what they believed. I don't know why this idiot kept trying to fight me when she honestly had nothing on me. I never said anything about her.

I didn't chase after a guy she liked–that I knew about. It was good old-fashioned jealousy. I could think about it without guilt, and it served her right to get slapped into reality. The world didn't revolve around her.

I, too, got slapped into reality and soon learned that my world didn't revolve around my plans, either.

Chapter 19

I was waiting for the ladies to come and get me. I had a feeling today would be drama, and although no one could be prepared for a fight, I was good to go as much as I could have been. I had never been to jail before, but likely, I was going for assault or something.

I heard the feet coming down the hallway as I tied my laces while sitting on the bed. The lady on the day shift said, "Kimmie, I need to see you right now." I replied, "Yeah, sure, alright." As I got up slowly from my bed and grabbed my backpack, she sat me down in her office and said, "I got some news for you, Kimmie, that I don't know how to tell you."

"What am I going to jail or something?"

"No, your grandmother just died."

"My grandmother? Are you sure you have the right girl? My grandmother died years ago."

"Oh, I am sorry, maybe I got it mixed up. Let me check the message." She looks down at a message note handed to her, likely by the receptionist. "Sorry, it says Jessica left a message for you. And she said to tell you her grandmother passed last night. Not your grandmother."

Just like that, my face went icy white. I am sure I looked like I had seen a ghost. This was worse than going to jail. Mrs. Bell was the person I had hoped to stay with when I got out of here. How could she just mysteriously up and die? How come I was the last to know she was this sick? I would have come to see her again if I only knew.

I didn't realize it, but I was screaming out of disappointment and shock. The lady who thought this was going to be a silent cry was in the shock of her life, too, as she held me. I released tears of sorrow on my birthday for the closest woman I had in my life to a mother. When I gathered my words, I asked for my phone, and she granted me the privilege.

I called Jessica, a number I had avoided like the plague. I cannot think of more than a handful of times I had called her usually in search for Mrs. Bell. She answered on the first ring. "Jessica, what is going on? Tell me this is some prank or joke."

"No, didn't mom tell you? She has been home in hospice for weeks now. They sent her home because they didn't know what else to do. She refused all the treatment options. She was always so damn picky. She thought God would save her when the doctors told her to–"

"She wasn't dumb, Jessica. She just told me she didn't want to live like that. Either God would heal her, or she was prepared to go."

"How can you say that? Don't you think she was a bit outside of her mind to go against the doctors? Why didn't you talk to her?"

"I did, but her mind was made up. We cannot tell her what to do."

Jessica starts crying. "I don't know what to do. I can't find my mom, and I am not sure how to do this. I really need your help."

"How exactly am I going to help you from in here?"

"I don't know, but we need to figure something out. We either need to call in a favor, or you need to break out."

"Give me a minute to get out of here so I can think. I will call you back."

"Don't you get it? I have to plan a funeral, and you are telling me you'll call me back!" They are asking me questions like what to do with her body. She is dead in the living room!"

"Look, I am a kid, and this is hard for me, too. Shut up so I can think, and I will call you back."

"Alright. You are right. We have to think. Call me back." I hang up not sure what to say or do. My hands are shaking, but if I break now, they are going to keep me here, and that won't solve anything for Jessica. Funny, I'm the one to have to calm down and wipe my tears so I can get out of here.

The lady came back and asked me, "Are you good?"

"Yeah, that was my friend. She lost her grandma, and the two of us are really close. She just needed someone to talk to."

"Okay, yeah. It looked like for a second she was related to you."

"Yeah, sorry; sometimes I see things that remind me of losing my grandma. It gets really intense. But I am good now."

"You sure you don't need a sick day?"

"Yeah, all good. Sorry."

"No need to be sorry. If you need me, I am here, you know?" I nodded my head yes, and she said, "Hurry up, or you are going to miss the bus."

I bolted out of that room and stopped by my bed one last time. I put what I couldn't live without, clothes, in my bag as quickly as I could. I hid the key to my stash under my pillow as I left. I am sure I wouldn't be back for one reason or another.

I got on the bus, keeping my head down. The tears couldn't be held back, but I needed to keep it together. I made it to school, looking for the only pair of eyes that could help me figure this out: Ariana. She wasn't in sight, so I headed to the bathroom.

I washed my face, and then I had to vomit. I don't know why vomiting seems to make me deal with trauma better, but it helps. After I threw up, I went back to the sink and tried to change the taste in my mouth. When I looked up, my guardian angel was near.

"Girl, where have you been?"

"Vomiting."

"You good? You look terrible."

"Mrs. Bell died."

"What?"

"Yeah, I got a message sent to The Home

today from Jessica. Mrs. Bell is gone. I just don't understand it, you know."

"Well, you know she was older, and a day like this was going to happen." She gave me a warm hug. I needed it again today. As I cried hard and she held me, I asked, "But why now? And today!"

"Awe, shit, it's your birthday. I am so sorry, Happy Birthday, Kimmie."

"Thanks. Turns out to be an eventful birthday." I sniffed and wiped away my tears because it was game time. "I need you to do me a favor..."

"Of course."

"Jessica is freaking out, and she asked me to help her with the funeral."

"Okay, but what are you going to do exactly?"

"I don't know. But Mrs. Bell died at home. I am not sure if the cops are there or what is going on. She died at home in the living room."

"Wait a minute. You want me to go and deal with a dead body, Kimberly?"

"I don't know what is going on, but I know I don't want to find out alone. I don't trust Jessica, and I need you."

"Look, I don't do dead people."

"Ariana, please. I really need you."

"Girl, I am failing math. You know I cannot miss a class."

"You're probably going to fail anyway. We can go to summer school together."

"This is crazy, but come on. I will get us a ride." Ariana asked a few students who she knew drove to school to give us a ride. She could be a bit scary when she wasn't sweet. We got to Jessica's house quickly, not sure of what we were getting ourselves into. I couldn't call the cops at the moment because I should have my black tail in school.

"What took you so long?"

"Please tell me you don't have a dead body in there, and nobody knows?" Asked Ariana.

"Of course not. She has a nurse. The nurse found her dead, but she is still asking me about funeral homes and things I don't know."

"Okay, I am sure Mom had something written up so we know what to do. Did she tell you where she has important documents?"

"She just shoved them in a drawer for the most part."

"Well, let's start looking." The girls start searching the drawers. Although Jasmine seemed pretty composed, everything she touched held her in a daze. Her tears are all cried out. Now, she has weird, beady eyes staring at me while I am trying to figure out what she is thinking.

I was getting frustrated as I looked because we were dealing with her mess and nonsense while we were grieving, too. She kept talking about stories of her and her grandmother when she was younger. The girl was full of regret, but she was a distraction. So I told her, "Look, Jessica, why don't you go and lay down so we can figure this out." She agreed, and away Ariana took her while I searched every drawer.

I made it to the kitchen drawers, and I couldn't believe it had taken us this long to find anything that could hint at Mrs. Bell's wishes. I opened her everything drawer, where she had condiment packages, bills, and important mail. As I pulled out the documents, a card with a lawyer's name on it was found.

I took my phone out of my pocket and dialed the number. "Hello, is attorney Samantha Ayers available?"

The lady on the other end said, "Who is calling?"

"Kimberly James."

"Do you have an appointment?"

"No."

"Give me a moment." She puts me on hold, and the music is comforting. I needed a soft soundtrack to help slow down the day. She comes back to the line and says, "I will patch you through. Please hold." I hold onto the phone, and a firm voice answers, saying, "Attorney Smantha Ayers."

"Hi, my name is Kimberly, and I am calling about Mrs. Bell."

"Mrs. Bell?"

"Yeah, she is an old lady who I think might be a client of yours. She died today." I started crying, but I held it together long enough for the attorney to confirm she was, in fact, a client of hers. I explained to her that she had died at home in hospice and asked her, "What do we do now?"

She told me she had the details for Mrs. Bell at her office and that I should come there as soon as I could. I gave Ariana the update, and she called the friend back to take us to the law office. The office was nice, big, and modern.

The same lady who spoke to me on the phone was likely the lady at the desk who greeted us. She welcomed us to the practice and walked us back to a conference room. I am not too sure if Samantha was expecting some teenagers to be in her office or not, but here we were waiting on her. I wasn't sure if I should have stood up when she entered or not, so we just sat there and awaited instructions.

She told us not to get up and to sit. We remained fixed to our chairs and looked at her to see what to do next. She said, "Thanks for coming, Kimberly."

"Yeah, of course."

"I know you are only fifteen, right?"

"Yeah."

"Do you have a guardian? Or a foster parent or something?"

"No, not at the moment. I am in a group home."

"Okay, technically, what I am telling you won't matter a whole lot because until you are eighteen, you won't be able to access what Mrs. Bell left to you."

"Excuse me?"

"Yes, you are part of Mrs. Bell's will."

"She had a will?"

"Yes, she made changes to it about a year ago. My instructions were to talk to you first and then Jessica."

"You sure?"

"Yes, I am paid for the details. The short answer is seventy-five percent of everything Mrs. Bell owns is yours. Her assets are listed in greater detail inside her will. Here is a copy of what she left you. And most importantly, here are her burial instructions."

"She thought about this early?"

"Yes, I am her estate planner. I helped her form the trust that you are listed as a member of. Your vote now is subject to her instructions, which I will manage until you turn eighteen. Some of what she requested, I cannot share until she said it was necessary."

"So, about the funeral?"

"Everything is in that envelope. She told me to give it to you, and you will take care of it."

"So what do I do if I have questions?"

"You have my card. Call me if you need me." She gave me another card, and this one had her cell phone number on it as well. I thanked her and immediately saved the number on my phone. I couldn't take the chance of losing it. We got up and walked out of the office. I thought about looking at what was in the envelope, but I should have waited until I at least got into the car.

I didn't look too hard at the numbers or the paper she showed me. I honestly was still fighting back tears and figured whatever she left me was a blessing because I didn't ask for anything. My mind right now was focused on Mrs. Bell's funeral arrangements. We got into the car, and as I sat in the backseat while the two of them talked, we drove to get something to eat.

I ordered a smoothie because today, I felt like that was the only thing I needed. Food I don't think I could keep down. I drank it as I read through the details and the letter.

"My Kimberly. Meeting you was the very best thing that could happen to this old woman. I don't know when you will read this, but I pray it won't make you sad. You have cried a lot, and I want this letter to bring you joy.

Know that you have been a daughter to me since the first day I laid eyes on you. I have always been determined to be here for you. You are a daughter I chose to have, and that makes you special. If I died quickly and without your knowing, it was only to protect you. Don't be mad at this old lady or yourself.

I love you, and you will always be part of

my heart. I do need to ask you for one last favor because I don't trust Jessica to do this. I need you to call the list of people in this letter, and they will handle all of the details.

Also, I have one last request, can you write and read my eulogy for the service? If you could write something for me, I would definitely appreciate hearing it. You were always good at making me smile. I am sure I will do it from heaven as well. All is well. If I am here on earth or gone on to glory, I am with God. This is only bye for now."

I close the letter and take a deep breath. How can this lady know a year ago that I would be here and able to do any of this? She planned her death and burial over a year and a half ago. Here I am struggling to think of a plan and she wrote me a to do list.

The letter and instructions were easy to follow so I did exactly what it said. I made the calls, and they asked me to be available to make the final selections. For some reason, I thought everything would just happen with the calls I made. But they each had questions about my preference. What flowers did I like? What color? What will the display look like? I was also asked about the casket and design.

I was getting overwhelmed, and I can say not having to deal with the price was a huge relief. I had no money, and I didn't know if she wanted to be cremated or buried. But thank God it was in the letter. She was so cool; she even had a limo car in her service package.

I knew Mrs. Bell was a classy lady, and she often wore white. So it seemed right to put her in white and make everything white. I think white was her favorite color because of how much she wore it.

Only in October would she wear a hint of pink, so I picked that as her second color. All white seemed to be a bit boring, too.

The day was winding down, and I knew curfew was coming. If you didn't have work, school, or a good reason to be past curfew, they were calling the cops to report you as a runaway.

I called the night shift worker, and thank God, it was the lady who gave me a cup of water many nights back. "Hey, this is Kimberly.--"

"Where are you? You know I am going to have to file you as a runaway in another hour."

"Yes, but I need you to do me a favor. Can you submit it as late as possible?"

"You know we are to report it at or by nine."

"I know, and I don't want to put you at risk of getting in trouble. But if you could please help me. I am dealing with a funeral, and I cannot come back. My friend is a mess, and I have instructions to follow to get everything together. I just don't want to let Mrs. Bell down."

"Look, I empathize with your situation, but you cannot skip curfew."

"I don't have a choice. If I come back, I will be on lockdown and will miss the funeral."

"Yes, you will be reprimanded if you miss curfew."

"Please, please, help me."

"I will do my best to push it off as long as I can. But you may have three to five days max."

"The funeral is on Sunday. They are releasing the body, and we have to go straight to the funeral home. So I should be well for about three days. That will work. Thank you!"

"Yeah, I gotta go do checks. Be careful."

"I will."

I thanked her one last time for buying me time, but I knew my clock started for when the cops would either come and pick me up or turn myself in. I am not even sure where I would go to do that. It's crazy. I have never committed a crime, but I feel like I have already been to prison, and I am skipping bail or something.

I couldn't think of the consequences because all that mattered was completing Mrs. Bell's final request. I had to write this eulogy, and it seemed to pull so much energy out of me. What do I say about a woman who lived to be like ninety-five years old? She knew everybody and everything. She was so kind and sweet, and she always made me feel at home. I loved this woman, and I wasn't sure what had made her choose me.

I only knew I was grateful to have known her. She was my angel, and I could only pray to express her character to the many people who knew her better than I did. I followed up about the program the next day so that the eulogy could be included in the program. The pastor and everyone were good about planning the funeral to be quick. We couldn't hold the body long because the morgue had a three-day policy, and the funeral home was full.

The church cleared the schedule for the weekend, so we can have her buried on that Sunday. I was doing my best to invite as many people as I could find from her drawers, and the church helped to invite her friends from church and wherever else. She didn't have a social media account. Making a post wasn't the easiest way. We had to go old school.

We had about fifty people confirmed to show up. I am thinking they all will not show up, so everything should be good there. I have been away from the girls home for a few days now, and I am just praying my luck doesn't run out until after I finish this funeral.

Getting to Sunday was tricky. I had to skip school the rest of the week because I wasn't sure if the cops would be looking for me. I stayed with Jessica, and she was doing okay, but she had several crying spells. I didn't see her as a mushy type, but death changes people.

I was in the kitchen doing what Mrs. Bell had done for me so many times. I made oatmeal. "Hey, you want any oatmeal?"

"Yeah, sure," replied Jessica. "But can you put bananas or something in it? I don't like it plain."

I cut up some bananas and added nutmeg and cinnamon like Mrs. Bell. I couldn't forget the butter and a pinch of salt to get it to taste just right. We sat at the table together, and we were cordial as we both ate our food. I would even stretch and say we were nice. I am sure Mrs. Bell was looking down on us from heaven, smiling.

I wasn't sure what Jessica was going to do now that her grandmother was gone, so I decided to ask. "So what are you going to do now with the house and everything?"

"I honestly don't know. I am supposed to speak with the lawyer and see what they say tomorrow after the funeral. I don't know if my grandma left me anything, let alone this house. Do you think it was paid off?"

"I think it was. But I don't know for sure. I am sure your grandma left you something."

"She loved you. But I am sure she just put up with me because we are family."

"Naw, she loved you too. She always talked about you."

"Yeah, probably to say how much of a pain I was?"

"No, she said you were talented and weren't living up to your potential."

"That sounds like grandma. So what are you going to do this morning?"

"I have a few last things to check on for the church, and everything should be good for the people to arrive. You should come to service today. You know she would love that."

"I will think about it. I am not big into church."

"See, it is a last request, and you will come. I gotta get dressed so I can arrive early. The church is sending the bus to get us. So if you coming, go change your clothes, and please take a shower." I held my nose in a joking way and laughed as I got up. She poked fun back by making a silly face as I walked away.

She didn't get up quickly but just sat there for a moment. I am sure this day was going to cement the truth for her like it was for me. Mrs. Bell, my second mom, and her grandma was gone. Surprisingly, she showed up at the door with clothes that were decent and clean.

She didn't do laundry, and I refused to be her maid. She had piles of clothes stacked up for when Mrs. Bell stopped washing or making her clean. She was really a junky person or lazy. Mrs. Bell told her about that all the time. When I got here, there were dishes in the sink and the floor was a mess, but I cleaned it like I did for Mrs. Bell.

I didn't mind helping out around the house; it was always the least I could do. For Mrs. Bell, it didn't seem like maid work; it was an act of love. She would give me a few dollars, too, afterward, but it was never about the money for me. I trust she knew that.

The bus got there to pick us up, and the driver made small talk. He was aware the funeral was today and said how he wished he could make it, but he had to work. I thanked him and said Mrs. Bell appreciated him trying to come and would understand. He teared up a little bit when he talked about remembering her in the church when he was young.

Mrs. Bell didn't play and was quick with popping children in Sunday school. "Back then, you could discipline children and tell their parents." He said when he got home, he got popped again for being disrespectful to her. He learned, like all the others, not to mess with Mrs. Bell.

That Sunday looked like Christmas at church. The church was packed, and it looked like the children Mrs. Bell taught from school came with their children. I wasn't sure how much food we cooked, because I was thinking only fifty people were coming. Maybe they all sent a message to the pastor or somebody to tell them they were coming.

This was my first time planning a black event, and I wasn't ready for the follow-through. I couldn't understand why so many people never told me that at least they were planning to come. Lesson learned! Always plan for the twenty or so people to show up who didn't RSVP to avoid a shortage.

I will lean on the church staff for later if all these people stay. The sermon that day was a light message on God's goodness. The pastor talked about how we need to trust God no matter what events befall us. We don't get to dictate His actions, but we can choose how we react to His direction.

I knew the message was for me. I didn't understand why Mrs. Bell had to die, although I knew someday she would. I guess deep down, none of us are really ever ready to say goodbye to those we love. Even those who treat their relatives and family like ghosts or terribly tend to cry at funerals and days like this, too.

There was something in my soul that said this message was for Jessica, but the more I listened, the more I realized it was for me, too. I have lost so many people I loved, and her death and my father's were both hard. I don't know what I would have done if she hadn't come with me to my dad's funeral.

Funny how I can hear her voice even now, and I trust it will be here when I attend her funeral later today. The day outside was sunny. Some of the cars left the parking lot after church dismissal, but most didn't. It was a packed house, and it didn't help that the pastor reminded everyone to stay after for her service.

I had to go in the bathroom immediately when I saw the hearse pull up. I knew Mrs. Bell was in there, and this would be my last goodbye. I hated goodbyes so much. I loved the warm memory flooding back to my mind of Mrs. Bell greeting me for the first time in this church. She was so kind and gentle–the version I knew. I am sure that as mothers turn to grandmothers and then great-grands, they get sweeter and sweeter.

Jessica used to joke that I had the better version of her grandma. She got the one full of rules. I think she saw that side because she needed it, like Mrs. Bell told me. Mrs. Bell was my buddy. She was more than a grandmother; she was my friend. I would be saying goodbye to my best friend today, but before I could cry, I was reminded to call Ariana.

"Hey, are you still able to make it?"

"Yes, I will be there. But I gotta tell you something."

"Yeah, what's up?"

"Oh, hold up,--" she starts to talk to someone on the phone, and at that moment, the pastor walked up to me. He said, "We are getting everything in place for the ceremony. Do you want to meet with Lady Jo so she can talk you through the walk-in?"

I replied, "Yes, of course." I got back on the phone, "Hey, Ariana, I am going to have to let you go."

"Yeah, of course, I will call you back."

"Okay, if I don't answer, I will see you here at church."

"Yeah, I will be there."

"It seemed like more details were being unloaded today than in the previous rehearsals. I was holding my breath whenever I walked near the casket. I didn't look inside, and I prayed they wouldn't open it too soon. I don't like looking at dead bodies at all. Too often, they don't look like the person you remembered anyway.

The music was turned on, and the people started to quiet down. Jessica, I couldn't find no matter how many times I walked around in the church and the bathroom. Did she escape out the back door or something? I went back to the front to see if she might have stepped outside, and I saw Ariana pull up.

As I walked toward her, I saw a familiar face in the car. "Hey, thanks for coming."

"Yeah, of course."

"Is that your dad?"

"Yeah, he came to my mom's today. They let him out early for good behavior. I wanted to tell you, but–"

"It's okay. It might never be a good time to let me know."

"I'm still sorry he came here. My mom couldn't take me, so it was him or nobody."

"It's all good." He didn't glance at me at all. He kept his head down and eyes forward after Airana got out of the car. He looked like he saw a ghost and wanted nothing to do with me. I was relieved. I didn't care to see his face ever again if the Good Lord made it so.

Arian and I went into the church together, and boom, we bumped into Jessica. "Where have you been?"

"I just needed a second." She didn't look the same as earlier today. Her eyes seemed a bit more stressed and pink. I'm not sure if she just had been crying so much or if she smoked, and I never noticed until now. When the coordinator came to us for the walk-in, it was apparent that Jessica wasn't completely sober because she kept asking the same questions over and over again. It was embarrassing. We had to form the line, and I asked Ariana to stand with me. She obliged, and the three of us walked down the aisle together, with Jessica walking up front. There were other people that started to fall in line after us, many people I had never seen before. I guess it is true. Family picnics and funerals are all that bring families together nowadays.

I had avoided the casket, but now there was no running, and yup, my fear; it was opened. We didn't do a wake, and I was so glad we didn't. But now I had to look at her. She deserved that, no matter how fearful I was. I walked, and my tears started to fall, but I was okay. Jessica made it to the coffin, and she stared at her grandmother for a good minute. She didn't cry or explode like I had thought she might.

She only touched her hand and whispered her final thoughts. When she turned to face us, her face told the story; she was very sad and needed a tissue. Someone had a box nearby and gave it to her. As she started to walk away, the guy with the box helped her get to her seat. She was hunched over when she sat down, and I am guessing the tears continued to flow.

I got to the coffin when Ariana nudged me to keep moving closer. I looked away before I looked down. When I looked at her, surprisingly, she looked like herself. Her face didn't seem to show any fear or pain for her passing, nothing like my grandfather or dad. She was an angel. My angel who would now be going to heaven to watch over me.

At her coffin, I said, "Mom, the only one I have ever known to show me love. Thank you for being so kind to me when I really needed you. You are still showing your heart to me now, and I am grateful. I love you, and I will never forget you. Please say hi to God for me and the angels. I pray God lets you visit my dreams sometimes." I barely got out the last line before I started to shake and cry.

Ariana grabbed me and kept me standing when I knew I would have sat down. She handed me the tissue. We both walked back to the bench, and I tried to collect myself. I am glad the eulogy was not first on the program because I wouldn't get a word out if it were.

I saw many people walk past her casket. Some left things inside it, but many walked away in tears. I prayed Mrs. Bell could see this from heaven. The service started, and it had a flow. I was watching, but my hearing wasn't a hundred percent the entire time. I drifted to the casket, then back to the speakers often.

Then Ariana nudged me, and I looked at her. She said they calling for you. That's when I realized they were all looking at me to come up. I asked Ariana, "Please come with me up there." She didn't argue but got up, and we walked together. I knew how much she hated being in front of an audience. I was glad I didn't have to coach her.

As I stood there, the words were blurry on the page. I started to read them, but when I saw into the casket again, my words got me choked up. Ariana knew I wouldn't recover, so she recited my eulogy for me. I was there standing with hot tears coming down my face. The room was quiet and the light somewhat dark until a corner door opened to let light in.

Two officers entered the church, but they stayed in the back. I knew they were there for me, but they didn't approach me. I prayed as I sat there for God to allow me to finish this. The service was nearly done, and we were about to walk the body out. I didn't want to walk again. I had made my peace already.

As they walked out with the casket out front, I followed behind as I was told. As the line went toward the exit, I saw the officers and walked over to them. They spoke frankly, "Kimberly James, you know we have to take you in?"

"Yes, I know. But if you could at least allow me to ride to the graveyard to bury my mom, I will come with no problem."

"This isn't how this works. When you get arrested, you leave now and in cuffs," the young cop said. He took out the cuffs in an attempt to cuff me, but the older cop stopped him.

"Chill, this is a funeral. I knew Mrs. Bell. We can wait until the funeral is over. But don't let me regret this, please."

"You won't. I am supposed to ride in the limo to the burial site."

"We will follow behind and stand off a bit for your privacy. We can give you about thirty to forty-five minutes tops."

"I don't know how long this will take, but thanks." I took a deep breath and said in my heart, thank you, Father, as I walked to the limo. I am walking in my prayer, and I am so grateful. It was nice to be driven to the site inside a limo. Mrs. Bell had class. The limo is white with chrome everywhere. I felt like a superstar getting out of the limo.

We walked a short distance to a tent with chairs. The green tarp was slightly lumpy, so I said a prayer for the ladies with tall heels on. My heels weren't high, so I wasn't scared, but for the ladies in attendance walking on stilts because their heels were so high they had trouble ahead. This was not an easy feat.

I quickly sat down, and the people filed in fairly quickly. I saw the officers off in the distance. The pastor conducted the ceremony and started to read from a guidebook. The talk was literally five minutes before he invited us all to either grab dirt or drop flowers into the open grave once the body started dropping down.

I tossed down three roses as I watched Mrs. Bell brought deeper into the ground. This was it, and I watched the process as another loved one, in a beautiful casket, was lowered beneath the earth. The pastor dismissed us and thanked us for our time. He invited us to come back to the church for dinner, but I knew I couldn't go.

Jessica didn't get inside the limo, and I didn't wonder why. She was running and hadn't been seen since the church dismissed. She acted like a vampire stuck in church. I looked up from the grave site, and I saw the cops standing and waiting. My palms were sweaty. All I had time to do was pray as I closed my eyes for a moment.

"God blesses those who work for peace, for they will be called the children of Yah (God)." Matthew 5:9

Dr. Lee has authored over thirty books across more than seven genres: adult, children, youth fiction, self-help, spiritual growth, novels, business, empowerment, etc. to help people in their most profound times of need.

She is also passionate about coaching programs and web courses she created for WAE (Write Anything Easily) Process, Embrace Your Crown, Turn Key Solution for Small and New Businesses, Transform Go Beyond Change (Personal Development, and The Lesson for youth and teenagers.

Connect and Shop my book

AuthorKLee.com

AuthorKLee.com
Creator of
WAE Process

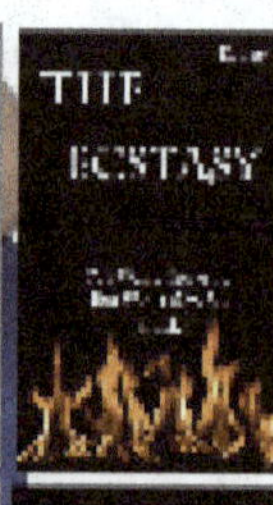

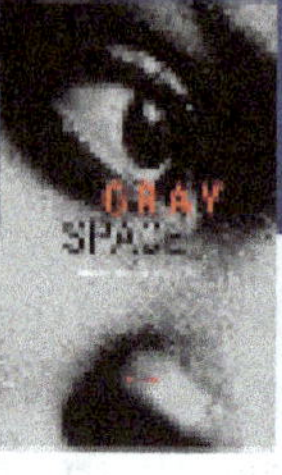

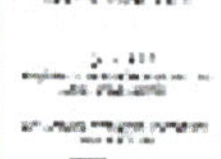

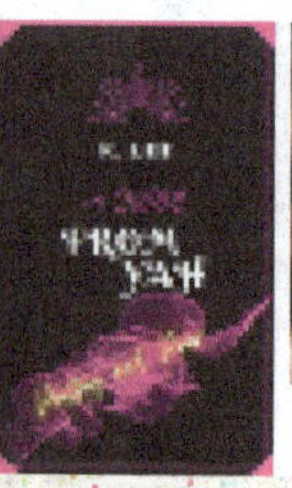
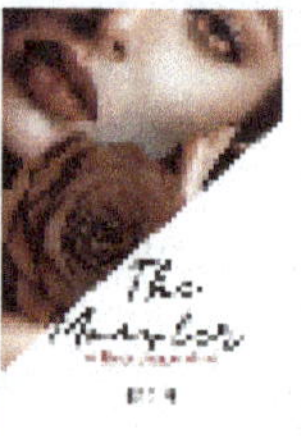
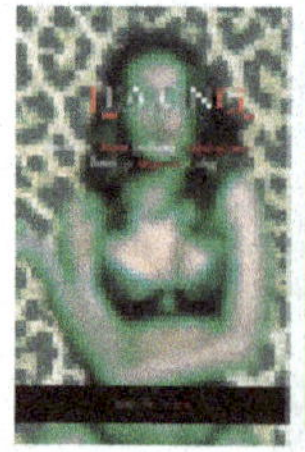

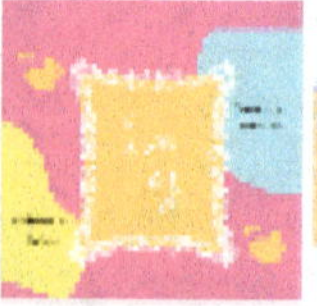

Explore and learn more about published authors affiliated with KLE.

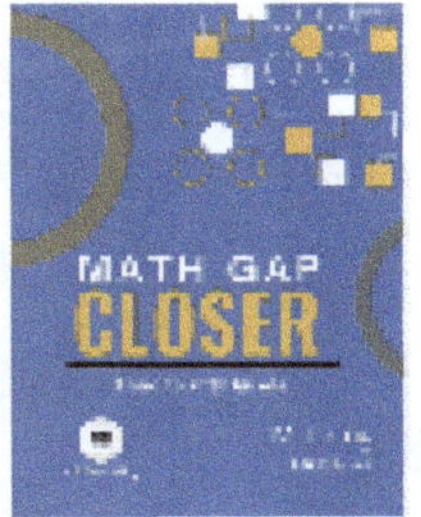

KLEPub.com

SCAN ME

Call or Text:
770-240-0089 Press Extension 1
Web: KLEpub.com
Email Services@klepub.com

It's time to start and finish **YOUR Story!**

KLE Publishing specializes in helping people become authors. In as little as 15 to 90 days, we can help you develop your books and e-books and publish to 39,000 outlets! We also offer audiobook services.

Write, Edit, Format, Publish
We can help from
Start to Finish.

Make My Heart Malt: A Romantic Comedy Sports Romance by Gia Stevens

www.authorgiastevens.com

Published by: Gia Stevens

Print ISBN: 978-1-958286-19-7

Editor: My Notes in the Margins, Davenport Edits

Publisher: Wild Clover Publishing, LLC

Cover Art: @aksi.art

v021626